CW1

After leaving school at fifteen, Mike Buckingham joined the RAF and served in the Middle East. Upon leaving the service in 1966, he worked for a succession of provincial newspapers as a reporter, before going to the University College of Wales, Aberystwyth, to take a degree in history. He is now a feature writer and columnist on the *South Wales Argus*. *Cwmikaze* is his first novel. Mike Buckingham lives and flies in South Wales.

MIKE BUCKINGHAM

CWMIKAZE

VISTA

First published in Great Britain 1999 as a Vista paperback
original by Victor Gollancz
Vista is an imprint of the Cassell Group
Wellington House, 125 Strand, London WC2R 0BB

A catalogue record for this book is
available from the British Library.

ISBN 0 575 60326 7

Typeset by SetSystems Ltd, Saffron Walden, Essex
Printed and bound in Great Britain by
Cox & Wyman Ltd, Reading, Berks

2 4 6 8 10 9 7 5 3 1

Chapter One

'JEEZIZ CHRIST, lookit that!' A couple of seconds later the blast waves hit the B–17G, bucketing it around the sky.

A section of rudder from the disintegrated bomber flew by making *Lazy Lady*'s pilot flinch.

One of the gunners was reciting a Hail Mary, shouting the words over the hammering of his gun and the metallic clatter of the shellcases cascading around his boots.

You never knew those guys in the other, dying Fortress and it wasn't going to happen to you. You'd been in the game too long. Too many tours of duty. How many times had your crew seen the beds opposite theirs stripped ready for another crew to replace the one that would never come back? Six? Seven times?

Keep closed up so the gunners can maintain a concentration of fire and keep flying the course and don't think about anything else.

As a boy the pilot had peered down into Lake Memphramagog and watched the silver fish under the landing stage turn as one and flee at the approach of a pike, exploiting their safety in numbers. That's what the huge bomber formation was doing now.

The Kraut fighters would get the inexperienced ones or the careless, or those that strayed from the bomber stream, but that wasn't going to be him because he wasn't any of those things.

Three summers ago was the last time he'd peered over the landing at the fish and that evening they'd driven into Burlington and got drunk because the next day he was going to the Army Air Force.

It was his favourite daydream and in dreaming it McNally, flying his little Piper PA–38 Tomahawk in the present day, had forgotten that the light was fading fast. The other B–17s in the formation slipped astern back into their own time-dimension, the co-pilot on the neighbouring aircraft in the formation waving a salute.

Once more he was alone in the pert little high-tailed plane three thousand feet over mid-Wales and slightly anxious as to the location of Maescwm Flying Club.

Propelling himself fully into the present he concentrated on getting his bearings and within ten minutes was able to make out the two hangars – one large, one smaller, and the cluster of lesser buildings around them.

'*Victor Yankee* clear to land, but you'd better be quick,' came the voice from the old tower.

'*Victor Yankee*. The light's not too bad,' McNally radioed back.

'I'm not talking about the light.'

His hand went automatically to the flap-lever giving the Piper half and then full flaps and taking off the power and feeling the increase in his heartbeat that always came before settling perfectly.

A bump, a rumbling, a touch of the brakes and then a sharp left turn towards the big hangar.

He stopped and put on the parking brake, ran the engine at 1200 revs per minute for thirty seconds before switching it off and, removing the key, checked the fuel and electrics were all off, set the trimmer at neutral, unbuckled himself, slid the seat back and climbed on to the wing and down on to the ground, enjoying the oily, hot smell of the aircraft.

The hangar at dusk was usually enough to set off another daydream. He often imagined it as it must have been, crowded with the camouflaged shapes of aeroplanes with ladders and trestles pushed up to them and men and women in overalls swarming over them like worker-ants. Cowlings laid aside to expose the viscera of pipes and wires, the sinews and arteries of the mighty fighting machines. Not tonight, though. The voice from the control tower had unsettled him.

Maescwm had never been a front-line flying base. Built just before the war for the training of pilots and navigators it had been used after 1941 and the entry of the United States into the war for the reception of dim-witted transatlantic pilots who thought Wales and Norfolk were pretty much the same place.

In the post-war rundown of the RAF, Maescwm had been almost forgotten. During the arctic winter of 1947 aircraftsmen who were careless about everything other than demobilization made nocturnal expeditions with axes and hewed away half the wooden billets for fuel for their own pot-bellied stoves.

The few huts that survived 1947 were seen off during the similarly bleak midwinter of 1963 and in the following spring the station was abandoned by the RAF.

Sheep, bats, birds and the occasional tramp had the run of the place until the formation of Maescwm Flying Club. The sheep had been chased out but the bats remained, rivalling the starlings McNally could now hear screeching in the hangar for roosting space, these the direct descendants of the wartime occupants.

He liked that. It lent a sense of continuity.

The latticed girders of the big hangar were encrusted with droppings and swifts nested under the corrugated steel eaves. The smaller hangar, which had been bolted and barred long ago, was the preserve of the bats. Nobody had been curious enough to check what was inside. Anyway, the keys had long since been lost.

Even before the RAF pulled out Maescwm had begun to settle down into a lazy torpor, cocooned by its remoteness and insignificance. The RAF had forgotten about it and it had forgotten about the RAF.

When the service finally relinquished control the old place creaked a sigh and settled down into the sleep of decades, happy to let the swifts, the bats and the starlings do most of the flying. There were now only six planes of varying ages and descriptions, including *Victor Yankee* in which McNally gave flying lessons. Crumbling and sleepy and almost completely passed over by great events, Maescwm Flying Club suited its members perfectly.

For them it was a delicious decay, the hangars peeling and becoming blotched with rust, weeds and grass forcing through even the thickness of the reinforced concrete. The clubhouse, which many years ago, as a briefing room, had been painted green for some long-forgotten commander-in-chief's inspection, had now faded to khaki.

Only one of the old station's buildings was spruce. Painted white and with trees and shrubs and a gravel path encircling it, it had been born again as the council-run Behavioural Orientation Language, Learning and Oral Experimentation centre. Once the officers' mess, it was the sole intrusion of the late twentieth century. ONLY SNOBS FLIE PLAINS had been sprayed in large red letters on BOLLOX's wall facing the clubhouse.

With a gathering sense of unease, McNally walked into a quietly murmurous clubhouse. Only Squadron Leader 'Dhobi' Thomas's voice could be heard distinctly.

8

'Bloody rum crew . . .' Dhobi was already lapsing into the staccato speech that signalled the despatch of his fourth large gin and tonic.

'Do you know what the co-ordinator, or whatever it is the crazed lesbian calls herself, said when I suggested her inmates should keep their literary endeavours to themselves?'

Dhobi's gin-pinkened eyes scanned the company, none of whom volunteered a guess.

'"For one fing they ain't inmates," she said. "They're clients and for annuver, it was the staff who wrote it. 'Ow do you expect us to meaningfully relate to the clients using the full paintbox of cognitive and communication skills if we can't spray on the fuckin' walls? Now piss off."'

The sound of a powerful four-wheel-drive pulling up made McNally look out the window to see Lawless, who gloried in the Christian names of Rospard Tintoretto and who claimed to have been baptized in an Italian brothel, shoehorning himself out of the driving seat.

Lawless was huge. Six foot three and wearing a double-pocketed blue shirt that looked as if it had been constructed from the sails of a windjammer.

Alice, his wife, diminutive beside him though tall in any other company also wore blue, a dress cut to expose the top of her breasts and flared to accentuate her extravagantly sculpted hips. She wore leather sandals and no stockings and her musky and expensive scent reeked of sin.

Lawless had chunks missing from his beard which could usually be taken as a good sign. It meant he was working well. From the way the car had slewed to a halt it was also apparent he had been drinking well. This was often a bad sign.

McNally guessed the couple had just come from Maescwm Workingmen's Club and Institute, an establishment several barstools short of a dive and favoured by

Lawless when assiduously applying himself to the problem of emptying a brewery. Lawless was a painter and a Fellow of the Royal Academy. He was also a self-proclaimed anarchist and had established himself as a vintage *enfant terrible* with the showing of his *Tripe-tych* at the Tate Gallery the previous summer, which had amazed the art world and baffled the paying public by the inclusion of the dried and varnished entrails of a goat.

McNally had once pointed out that it was hard to be an *enfant terrible* in one's fifties, an observation that had earned him a glower of sufficient force to down a Lancaster bomber.

'Heard the news?'

The bits missing from his beard made Lawless look comical and threatening at the same time. The clipped-away tufts had been made into paint-brushes, a saving he had adopted during the execution of *Tripe-tych.*

It would be interesting to know what Lawless was up to now and whether it would stink as badly as its predecessor. He'd have to ask Alice, if they ever got back on speaking terms.

'Let me guess. The Italians have found your birth certificate and you're not a bastard after all.'

It was the sort of crack that had an equal chance of being rewarded with a slap on the back or a crack on the jaw.

McNally, who liked occasionally to pummel Lawless's elephantine ego, guessed the former. Anyway there would be plenty of time to see the punch coming and duck.

The big man grinned, emptied his tankard at a swallow, belched and put his arm around Alice under her armpit giving her left breast a proprietorial squeeze.

'Wrong, McNally, you witty little Irish fucker. This concerns a much bigger bastard than me. Ever heard of a bloke called Snilesworth?'

Another pint disappeared with Vesuvian gurglings. Lawless swept bits of foam out of his moustache and belched again. Alice was looking straight at McNally with a malicious glint. She's the one who's got it in for me, he thought. Not her big slob of a husband. Any real trouble and it's going to come from her.

'No.'

'You will. Ephraim Snilesworth. A Yorkshireman with all the personal charm of an anvil. He's the club's new landlord as from a couple of hours ago. I imagine your eviction notice will arrive any time within the next month.'

Lawless smiled, a sight that was not unlike suddenly coming across a row of broken tombstones in a thicket.

'Bad news for the club. Its only redeeming feature is that it causes you deep personal distress.'

It was indeed news to make the brow sweat and the scrotum shrivel. McNally turned to Dhobi, the club's treasurer, secretary, chairman and just about everything else.

'Afraid so,' the older man murmured into his glass.

'The decision went through the council's planning committee this afternoon. Snilesworth's made a killing in the north and now the bugger's got us squarely in his sights. A subsidiary of Dreemidwell Homes, his property company now looks almost certain to snap us up from the council which is technically our landlord. We're going to be a retail park. Virtually signed and sealed. Christ help us!'

'The clubhouse? Hangars? My hut? it all goes?' McNally was aware of his voice sounding pathetic and lost.

'All going. All except BOLLOX. Snilesworth clinched the deal by promising to extend BOLLOX and fund it for five years. That got the Labour councillors on his side.'

'Bastard.'

McNally felt the term didn't do people like Snilesworth justice but it would have to serve. He'd never even met the man but knew the sort. People like him and the world they were remorselessly creating had driven him into the sanctuary of Maescwm Flying Club in the first place. Now he had been run to earth, cornered by the joyless twentieth century and its obsession with supermarkets and fast-food joints. Dry stores and garden centres, conformity and computers.

'Bastards.'

Lawless sank a third pint and with his arm still around Alice swayed out amid a ragged chorus of 'Goodnights'. Alice prudently grabbed his ignition keys.

McNally pumped Dhobi for information, hoping for a crumb of comfort. Somehow the man in the blazer and RAF tie – the joint founder-member who had come to symbolize the club – looked much older than before.

Snilesworth, the stealthy predator for whom peace of mind was something to be snatched, had entered Dhobi's world like a fox in a chicken coop.

There was no comfort to be had.

'Sorry, old boy. Short of a miracle, that's it. Our number's up.'

McNally left the clubhouse and walked across the perimeter track along the path beaten through the long grass to the old dispersal hut which was now his home.

Somebody had been there. A light he was sure had been switched off was burning.

And there was another clue.

MCNALLY YOU BASTARD was sprayed all over the front door and since the spelling was correct it certainly couldn't have been by anyone from BOLLOX.

He knew who it was, all right, and she must be in a towering rage over last night.

What a day.

What a god-awful bloody day!

Chapter Two

McNally didn't mean to be a bastard to women. It had just historically worked out that way. Usually he blamed the socially retarding effect of service life.

He had spent nine years in the general engineering branch of the RAF before being discharged more or less honourably with the rank of corporal. His job had been to maintain the starter trolleys, hydraulic rigs and compressors needed to service aircraft on the ground. It wasn't the most glamorous job but he had relished the magic of the aircraft.

His squadron's planes were Handley-Page Hastings, workhorses built with wartime technology, which, because of their ruggedness and simplicity, saw service right through the Berlin airlift and the demands of a 'palm and pine' air force lumbering on into the late 1960s. The old planes were powered by four Hercules engines the age of which was demonstrated by the streaks of oil below the nacelles. An archaic tail wheel which put their blunt, bossy noses twelve feet above the tarmac was the plane's eloquent two fingers up to the jet age.

He had loved them, and had frequently volunteered to help the engine and airframe fitters who were the acolytes serving the silver monsters. With variously numbered *Air Publications* as their bibles they had crawled into the belly of the beasts and he had become initiated into the holy and complex rites enacted amid the myriad pipes, wires, valves, rods, levers and switches that kept the old planes airborne.

McNally had many times sat in the pilot's seat far above the concrete dispersals and vowed that one day he would fly. Like ninety-five per cent of the RAF he had been unable to do it in the service but once out of the main gate with discharge papers in his hands and a severance cheque in his wallet he had blown the lot on flying lessons. He had been broke ever since, a state of affairs that had stifled any grandiose plans he might have entertained as far as women were concerned.

Alice Lawless, to be fair, hadn't made many demands upon his purse. Just his sanity. Which was understandable, because she needed all the sanity she could get.

The odd thing was that apart from an occasional drunken eruption, Lawless seemed unperturbed by the fact that McNally was sleeping with his wife. In fact McNally suspected that the artist rather enjoyed allowing what he considered a lesser mortal to drink from the deep wells of his personal charity.

Peremptory and half-pissed leg-overs after encounters in bars from Hamburg to Hong Kong had not really prepared McNally for the tricky situation that had begun to develop within a month of his arrival at Maescwm.

When the signals first started getting through to him Alice had been by herself at the club bar wearing the sort of tailored slacks that forced other females to make grudging but appreciative remarks and men to dribble.

A deep-blue cotton shirt was unbuttoned to her cleavage, a warm and sweet-scented area dusted with tiny freckles. Small creases appeared or disappeared as her breasts moved but elsewhere her skin was luminescent, taunting the years.

A reddish tinge to the hair and blue eyes gave an

impression of Irishness but the finishing-school accent with a throaty timbre had Cheltenham as its westernmost limit and the eyes were not laughing, but coldly challenging.

By the time McNally discovered that she was devoid of morals and totally self-absorbed it was too late.

He shifted in his bed in the old dispersal hut which was now his home and stubbed his cigarette in the ashtray made from the top of an aero-engine piston. A stirring in his groin might soon need some quelling. Mad Alice might be. Immoral and feckless she certainly was. But she plucked the reckless, lonely chord right at the centre of his being. He had observed the way she worked on him, diminuendo at first, artfully displaying the turn of a wrist or the flick of her hair, then glancing to see its effect. Moving up through the sexual register with lingering eye contact, she would place her head close to his so that he could see her breasts and finally a hand softly squeezing his forearm and a remark breathed in a deep, sensual voice had him digging his fly-buttons out of the ceiling.

The most shattering climaxes to this orchestrated assault upon the senses came when Lawless was with her. He'd had a hint of that last night. She could have men fighting over her like rutting stags. It was part of her nature, deep and powerful and darkly sexual, beyond morals. Testing one man against another and weighing up their potential as fighters or hunters. Woman's most ancient privilege.

This woman was an out-and-out tart and he loved it. In fact he would love it right now but she would be at home with Lawless, giving her husband a blast of the searing sexual energy he had sampled last night before their fight.

He tried to imagine the scene. Lawless would be painting her, but she wouldn't be in one of the classically coy poses. Not Alice. It would be something unimaginably crude, wickedly brazen and sluttish. The honey-trap for which they all fell. It was her way of challenging the world. The

15

aching in the loins was now in dire need of quenching. His hands reached down.

BRRINGG, BRRINGG. BRRINGG, BRRINGG.

'Hello, treasure,' the voice cooed.

It was Hollywood.

He lay back and let his pulse get back to normal.

'What are we up to today? Salivating at the thought of that awful, lascivious Lawless woman, I shouldn't wonder,' said the voice.

Hole in one.

'Not even close.' He remembered the sprayed message on the outside of his door which still had to be expunged.

'Just thinking about doing some housework.'

'Likely story. Now listen. Why don't you put your feather duster down and slip your pinny off and come for a nice little latchlifter at the Wrath of Grapes? A teensy-weensy early morning snorter and then we'll go to my place and I'll unravel your knotted muscles. You're all worked up over that woman. I can tell.'

'Sounds wonderful. In fact there's only one thing stopping me from skipping the drink and heading straight down to your place for a massage and whatever might follow.'

'Tell me and I'll make it right for you.'

'You're a bloke. Gay as a ton of carnival bunting. Witty, amusing, possessing all the skills of allurement and seduction. But a bloke. Bent as a docker's hook.'

'Oh, fiddlesticks. You're just an old square,' Hollywood said in his best pouting voice.

'A definite affirmative on the drinks front, though. Shall we say half an hour?'

'Super!' Hollywood trilled. ''Bye, treasure.'

Hollywood must have been calling from the Wrath of Grapes. By the time McNally got there two empty glasses containing the debris of cocktails were in front of his friend and a blue cocktail cigarette was smouldering in an ashtray containing the colourful butts of five others. Three proletarian youths sitting at a table opposite were sniggering and snatching looks at Hollywood that contained a mixture of amusement, curiosity and latent hostility.

'You see the one who's glowering at me?' Hollywood shot the question before McNally could even say hello.

'He's gay. I can tell the way he's stealing looks when his mates aren't watching. Little minx.'

McNally blanched inwardly. It happened quite a lot. Hollywood was in one of his aggressively queer moods.

'I like the coat,' McNally said in an attempt to draw Hollywood's attention away from the boy. It seemed indecently early for gay flirtations. Gay didn't feature much in Maescwm's cultural landscape, anyway. It was a word still used in the local newspaper to describe flower arrangements at the annual show.

'Not very . . . uh . . . Maescwm, though.'

The loose-fit jacket was of pale-blue watered silk with wide shoulders and went with his eyes. Hollywood was wearing white slacks with expensive leather sandals and lemon-coloured socks, also silk and the whole ensemble complimented his tan. On the French Riviera it would have been chic. But in Maescwm, where clean jeans were considered swish, it was an invitation to a punch-up.

Hollywood liked to live dangerously.

'My God, what is!' He dragged down the corners of his mouth and put on an imploring expression.

'Don't you think he's nice?' Hollywood waved his cigarette in the direction of a scowling youth. 'I like a bit of grit in my diet from time to time. D'you think he's noticed me?'

'No, I shouldn't think so.' McNally gave a short laugh. 'You melt into the background so unostentatiously. He probably thinks you're the village blacksmith unwinding after a hard day's beating ploughshares and meddling with horses' hooves. You are about being noticed. Being noticed is what you do best.'

Hollywood had been born Alaun Jones, the son of a Rhondda colliery manager, although nobody in Maescwm ever called him that. His nickname was an expression of his most passionate interest.

Hollywood was twelve years older than McNally and had done his national service in the Royal Artillery. It was a period of his life rarely spoken about but McNally still smiled at the recollection of Hollywood's first mention of it.

'Can you imagine it, treasure?' he had asked in his best camp style, the lyrical tenor in him trilling away. 'Me lumping those great bullets around! I told them it played hell with my nails but would they listen? I asked for a transfer to the Navy and this silly bitch of an officer asked me why. "Why?" I said. "Those ducky-blue uniforms are so much more *me*." I plucked at the horrible lumpy khaki costume they'd given me but he couldn't see the point. Made my life a living hell after that, they really did.'

Hollywood's sniff had dismissed the entire Royal Corps of Artillery.

'Let me get you a drink.'

The scowling youth was showing signs of extreme agitation. Probably trying to assemble the words 'off', 'fuck', 'poof' and 'you' into the right order.

McNally had good cause to remember the night a very drunk Hollywood had tried to chat up a miner in a late-night Cardiff drinking club and devoutly hoped there would be no repetition.

'I'll get it.' Hollywood flashed a smile at the boy who, from his concentrated frown, seemed to be experiencing thoughts, their passing marked on his brow like ships on a hitherto uncharted ocean.

'Sit down, you raving fruitcake,' McNally urged. 'I'll get it.'

'Spoilsport.'

When Hollywood's father had retired the family moved to Maescwm where his mother opened a card shop. When she died Hollywood had taken it over, creating for himself at the back a cosy little parlour where he kept his collection of old-time music-hall records and song sheets, several nineteenth-century watercolours and engravings of North African and Levantine landscapes, several hundred film biographies and encyclopedias, a smelly cat called Saddam and the last lingering shreds of ambition about one day being discovered by the movie industry.

The price of friendship with Hollywood was high.

Discounting drinks and cigarettes, of which Hollywood consumed enormous amounts, it had already cost McNally one broken nose rescuing him from a throttling at the massive hands of a Newport steelworker and many nights in lost sleep consoling him after fractured love affairs.

In return McNally got a friend who fed him hot meals during his occasional drinking bouts and slipped him odd bits of cash when pupil pilots were a bit thin in the air. He also acted as McNally's agent, through which his very few dealings with the world outside Maescwm were conducted. And since he paid no tax and received no state benefits, the latter was in practice restricted to cashing cheques and providing a poste restante address.

Hollywood was one of relatively few people who knew of McNally's home, snuggled away in the lee of an old bunker near the perimeter of Maescwm's airfield.

After fifty-five years, Hollywood's face was beginning to resemble the ancient temples in one of his North African landscapes. Classical, but crumbling fast. Even now his ambitions in cinema might well have been realized had he not been utterly incapable of playing a straight part.

'Trouble with women, is it?' asked Hollywood when they were settled with their drinks. 'Not surprised. She's trouble, that one you've picked. I always said so.'

McNally outlined the argument of two nights before and told Hollywood about the spray-can attack on his home. Hollywood just sipped his drink and smiled with amusement.

'Got you properly by the love-nuts, hasn't she? Married too, you dirty little toad. Mind you, I imagine she's a bit of a handful. Her poor old man probably appreciates your help. When she comes in the shop she goes for Modigliani reproductions and the occasional Paul Klee. They're the worst, the Modiglianis. All that decadence.'

In Hollywood's world people were characterized by the sort of greetings cards they bought.

'Before last Christmas she came in for black wrapping paper. 'Yes, you little trollop,' I said to myself. 'I know what's on your mind.'

It was McNally's turn to smile. His treasured Rayban sunglasses had arrived wrapped in black paper.

'I get horny just thinking about her. She's the perfect sexual animal. You could examine her least erotic part, the hard skin at the back of her heels, and be moved to poetry. Unless you've felt her wedding ring cold against your—'

'Yes. All right. Don't go on,' Hollywood shrilled in mock alarm.

'Ah, but her soul. It is as black as night at one moment and bright and pure as an April's day the next. At the moment it is dark. An abyss into which I peer with trepidation, sensing the dark and fecund forces writhing below.'

'O gawd! You sound like a half-cut D. H. Lawrence. Give it a rest and shag someone else for a bit.'

'You're joking. She's completely irrational when it comes to affairs of the heart. She can be at it like a bitch in season but if I played away she'd cut my wanger off and serve it cold for supper. The mad cat has already sprayed a rude message all over my hut. Now she's all over her husband. Doubtless she'll send me pictures of them engaged in some sublime perversion.'

Hollywood pursed his lips.

'I think we'd better speak about the sale of the airfield before you make a sticky mess on the seat. A councillor who's a friend of mine told me about it. Compared with the problem posed by the sale of the airfield, McNally, the woman is meaningless. If the airfield goes, your whole way of life goes with it. Say cheerio to your home, your job and your anonymity. Say hello to some seedy bedsit, extended periods of self-abuse and the taxman. As things stand I don't envy you. Snilesworth, your tormentor, is a cold and ruthless man. Without passion or poetry. English.'

The word 'English' was drawn out and concluded with a look in McNally's direction which carried a hint of accusation. Liverpool Irish was still English as far as Hollywood was concerned. The ancient enemy, feared and hated.

'Anyway, I think your problems are connected.'

Hollywood assumed a faraway look and blew a long stream of smoke at the ceiling. The three youths were drinking up and leaving. The neanderthal one looked as if he was struggling to remember the insult he'd been rehearsing for the last quarter of an hour.

'All right. I'll take the bait. What's the connection between Alice and Snilesworth?'

'Didn't you know? Oh, poor dear. He's screwing her.'

McNally took a long pull of his pint and replaced the glass on the table with a shaking hand. The two-timing little bitch. A delicious rush of jealousy surged through him. He lit a cigarette and drew the smoke in deeply, letting the sweet pain mix with the hit of nicotine.

'How do you know?' He tried to keep his voice level. In his mind's eye he saw the wanton Alice writhing on the bed, Snilesworth taking off his trousers, folding them along the creases and hanging them over the back of a chair. Alice popping a couple of pills and him spraying male fragrance under his armpits. Her pulling at the waistband of his immaculately white underpants. Snilesworth, the puritan, smirking, dismissive of the woman yet drawn by her. Something he must possess . . .

'A friend told me. We gossip a lot in my circle. Gays always know when someone's having it off.'

There was a loud 'splat' on the window opposite them and conversation halted out as they watched the contents of the bowels of an incontinent seagull slither down the window.

'Not my bloody week, is it?' said McNally. 'My woman thrusting hot pokers of jealousy inside me and the immediate prospect of no flying, no home and no job. Why does my piece of bread always drop jam-side down?'

'That,' said Hollywood, 'is unforgivable self-pity. For God's sake, do something about it,' and he put on the air which said that in matters of the heart and in practical matters of survival he'd forgotten more than McNally would ever know.

'Like what?'

'Well. It seems to me that if you manage to save the flying club she'll come running back agog at your machismo. They always do. Especially when they think you're doing it for them. I can see me in the part, actually. All tough and determined. Like Barbara Stanwyck in *The Cattle Queen*.'

'Except that Snilesworth owns the town bank and can afford to hire the gunslingers. He's a pillar of society and I don't even officially exist. And he's just breezed into town and stolen my gal. I know a man's gotta do what a man's gotta do. The only problem is I don't know what the hell it is this particular man is supposed to do.'

'Surprise her. Do something out of the ordinary.'

Hollywood was staring intently at the grey and white guano still sliming down the window as if gaining inspiration from it.

'Like what?'

'Bomb him.'

A silence. 'I don't follow.'

Hollywood blew smoke down his nose and regarded McNally much as he would have a student in BOLLOX's remedial class in cognitive skills.

'Bomb him. Tie a bomb to that aeroplane of yours and drop it right in the middle of Snilesworth's offices and blow his nasty little empire to smithereens.'

'Don't be so bloody daft.'

'What's daft about it? I can see you now like one of those handsome Japanese pilots in the war, tying a headband with funny letters all over it around your forehead and climbing into your plane with weeping girls and clouds of drifting orange blossom all over the place in preparation for the last, desperate, brave but ultimately futile gesture. What do they call those geezers?'

'Kamikaze pilots.'

'Mmm. We'll have to give it a Welsh flavour. How about Cwmikaze? That could be the code name for the mission.'

McNally looked unbelieving.

'This is lunacy. It might happen in films but not in real life. You are stark, staring mad.'

Hollywood had been trying to catch the reflection of himself in the window opposite and at first appeared not to hear.

'Only up to a point,' he said, turning to McNally with a devastating smile.

Chapter Three

Sanity was clearly on the ebb tide.

'Bomb . . . him?' McNally asked weakly.

'Bomb him.'

'With an aeroplane?'

'Exactly,' Hollywood said impatiently.

'Isn't that what the noisy things are for?' He made a sweeping gesture which managed to suggest flight but also absolute dismissal of any objection to his idea.

There was one great central truth about his friend, McNally reflected, once it dawned upon him that Hollywood was in deadly earnest and found himself beginning to contemplate the mad grandeur of the concept. Once Hollywood's mind locked on to something it was as hard to shake off as a Stinger missile. The bombing plan was glorious in its simplicity; so obvious that nobody except Hollywood could have thought of it. Only a person of screaming theatricality could have hatched this one.

'Not always. Relatively few are made for bombing and they tend to belong to the government. Governments are funny like that. They like bombing people themselves but hate freelances getting involved.'

Hollywood shrugged. 'There you are. I make a perfectly sensible suggestion and all you do is pick holes.'

He slid a ten pound note towards McNally. 'Go and fetch the drinks. That's all you're bloody good for.'

McNally went to the bar and returned with a cocktail and a pint which he placed in the centre of a beer mat upon which had been printed the details of a competition.

Even in the RAF he'd never filled out any form he didn't have to. McNally's imagination was haunted by a giant computer controlled by a government or big business or some other malign outfit wanting to run his life for him.

Even competitions printed on beer mats were potential traps. You filled in your name and address, telephone number and postcode and before you knew it you were on somebody's computer. Governments bought computer lists from businesses and vice-versa. Even the most innocent-seeming appeal for information held a catch.

'Anyway, our plans are quite unsuitable. The Piper has got low wings making downwards visibility a problem and the Cessna . . .'

'And the Cessna—?'

McNally shook his head, instantly alarmed at the fact that he was actually beginning to weigh up the possibilities in his own mind. His own grasp on sanity was slipping. With its wings above the pilot's head leaving a clear view of the ground the old Cessna could indeed be used to drop a bomb. Oh, God. A little inner voice, his leprechaun, was beginning to warm to the idea. There might be madness in the method but there was method in it.

'OK. All right. I grant you it might be possible to drop a bomb from a Cessna. But somebody is bound to notice a light aircraft lining up on a target and lobbing a few pounds of high explosives overboard. There'd be a bloody great explosion for a start which would wake up half the county. I like your style, you old sod. It's a great plan which should be in a film. But it's utterly and completely bonkers and if you don't mind me saying so only a raving fruitcake like you could come up with it. Am I coming through loud and clear?'

'What *is* coming through is an apparent inability on your part to think laterally,' Hollywood sighed deeply.

'Pearls before swine, I say. You come to me with problems and I give you solutions. If you don't like what I have to say then why bother to ask? It would work. I've seen 633 Squadron and the Dam Busters and that dishy guy who played Guy Gibson VC. That's how they did it. They had sort of big cargo compartments with the bombs in and a little plane went ahead and dropped flares over the factory they were supposed to be targeting. There's always lots of flock.'

'Flak.'

'Is that the lovely sparkly stuff? Anyway. Usually the bombs wouldn't drop when they pulled the toggle or whatever it's called and then some poor boy got the job of prodding the release catch with a ruler or something. Then one of the chaps firing the guns shouts "Focke Wulf!" and this little plane zooms out of the blue and shoots at the RAF one and hurts one of the lovely blond boys wearing a rather fetching sheepskin jacket and blood starts oozing out from under it. While all the other planes made it back to base this one is trailing behind with lots of black smoke pouring out the back. Then, just as the people in the control tower are about to give up there's a stuttering drone in the distance and the crippled plane comes limping in with the dawn. All the fire engines and ambulances race out to it and they lift the injured men down and a lovely WAAF embraces the blond boy and you can see they're going to get married. That's the only bit I don't like.'

'It's an . . . uh . . . interesting idea,' McNally said slowly. 'How did it cross your fertile mind?'

Hollywood pointed up at the pigeon shit on the window.

'I'll get the drinks this time.' Hollywood drained his and sashayed towards the bar. One or two drinkers smiled good-naturedly. Others looked on in wonderment. It wasn't often you got a free floor show in the Wrath of Grapes.

Hollywood chatted with the barman showing no signs of having just suggested a crime which was tantamount to an act of war within one's country, a treasonable offence for which you could still very probably be hanged, drawn and quartered.

It was spring when McNally loved Maescwm Flying Club most, the warm, blowy days with the cumulus towering like ghostly icebergs in a silent and limitless ocean. Meadow flowers amid the tall waving grass releasing their sweet oils to the sun. Savouring it with a cool drink in his hand, sitting outside the clubhouse or his hut gradually easing the pressures on his inner ear which came after a flight. From the first day he landed a job as chief (and only) flying instructor, maintenance fitter, publicity officer, security man, health and safety officer and occasionally even bar steward, McNally felt he'd won a ticket to live in his own dream.

The old air-raid shelters and grassy dispersal bunkers were crumbling year by year and would soon be like the grassy burial mounds left by the first Welshmen. The airfield's huts and the hangars likewise faded and settled imperceptibly on their foundations with each year that passed. It was a slow and gentle decay but it provided the mulch that nurtured his nostalgic senses.

Summer was a good time too, when the sun warmed the clubhouse still painted in its drab grey-green camouflage, and members sat outside listening to the varying pitch of piston-engines as planes taxied and took off and landed amid the insect-like drone of distant ones: the smell of aviation gasoline, and the way the crepe soles of his desert boots became tacky when he walked in a puddle of spilled fuel were all part of it.

He flew when somebody wanted a lesson and when he

had the money for fuel he flew just for the fun of it. Most of the time he liked simply to potter on the ground, painting a piece of equipment, driving the fuel bowser or earning an extra couple of pounds by washing a member's plane.

The RAF had left behind an ancient generator used for providing power to large aircraft while they were being serviced or started up and which was similar to equipment he had maintained in the RAF. At Maescwm it was practically useless but he took pride in keeping it in perfect condition just the same. He liked to tow it to within striking distance of the club bar and clean the curburettor on the old Ford 100E side-valve engine or sometimes grind in the valves or add a lick of paint where the weather had got a hold.

When he wasn't doing that he was often to be found under his rickety old Morris Minor Estate which he'd run on to a ramp improvised from the brick foundations of an old airman's hutment. About fifty per cent of his income came from fixing members' cars.

How far would he go to protect this way of life? He knew the answer to that already – as far as he could without fear of detection, without his shell of secrecy being pierced.

Faced with the threat presented by Snilesworth he could either fight or run. He had no particular objection to running away – the last fifteen or so years of his life had been an escape – but the only point in running was if you had a place to hide.

He didn't. Only Maescwm provided the haven. He was too old for the RAF even if they'd have him back. Anyway, he'd done with rules and discipline and it was never a good idea to go back to a place you had once loved. He might be able to get a job with a commercial airline or at an aircraft plant where he would be the smallest of cogs in a huge, impersonal machine. Anyway the modern aircraft he'd been working on interested him hardly at all. Avionics, as they now called it, controls operated by computers, a slick and slimy word which stank of the boardroom.

'Flying' was the proper term, or 'aviation'; workman-like, practical words smacking of oil and warm aluminium wings, the grubby and fraying braided material on control columns and the buffeting heat from roaring engines and the breathless moment when you come in with a rush to land.

McNally snapped out of his mental meanderings and touched down back in the Wrath of Grapes.

'This Snilesworth. Where does he live?' he said, coming out of his dream.

Hollywood smiled. McNally was sniffing the bait.

'You'll have seen it from the air. A lovely old place with a Paladian front five miles out of town on the Brecon Road. Private fishing, which is handy from your point of view.'

'Why? I'm not interested in fishing.'

'I know, but the river is a superb landmark, particularly at night when there's a bombers' moon.'

McNally remained expressionless as Hollywood pressed on.

'There's a huge rectangular building behind the house, all metal and glass. That's the nerve centre of Dreemidwell Homes, Snilesworth's development company where all his printed and computer records are kept. It's called his bunker. Knock that out and it would be ten years before his affairs are back into any sort of order. You would save the airfield and win Alice's adoring attentions for ever.' Hollywood wrinkled his nose ever so slightly. 'For what that's worth. Think about it.'

Hollywood shot a glance, sensing that McNally was weighing up risks and technical difficulties. What he had proposed was pure theatre, a passionate drama designed to appeal to the Irish in the eccentric man.

The idea was up and running full speed. All he had to do was to get in with the clincher.

'Besides. It's where he takes your girlfriend for nookies, isn't it? Worth levelling the place for that alone. Purely from your own individual perspective, of course.'

Hollywood lit another cocktail cigarette and sat back to watch McNally's face turn a fighting red and a tiny vein on his temple begin to throb. 'I mean.' Hollywood picked up the wet beer mat and with the faintest of inward-directed smiles began peeling off the competition details.

'It's not as though any computer's got tags on you. You've got the perfect alibi.

'You simply don't exist.'

Chapter Four

After sex with Lawless or McNally Alice felt warm and sleepy as though each of her joints had been eased loose and laid out in the sun. After Snilesworth she felt exercised.

They had eaten at a French restaurant much patronized by businessmen and the country set. A few had acknowledged Snilesworth as they escorted their wives or mistresses to candle-lit tables. Snilesworth's eyes had followed them as they took their seats, logging them into his mental computer.

He drank bottled mineral water with his meal.

The strange thing about Snilesworth, she decided, was that there was almost nothing strange about Snilesworth. He was ordinariness taken to an extraordinary degree.

Flamboyance in his clothing was confined to a splash of primary colour in his silk tie. Everything else was light grey, right down to his socks.

Maescwm Flying Club was the tacitly acknowledged black hole of the evening, a subject so all-pervading that neither wished to speak of it although it hovered around the table like the ghost of a starved waif.

Snilesworth was too loud in ordering the food and her wine. Alice, at odds with herself, found this endearing in a childish sort of way. He ate like a dog snapping at flies. There was a certain blamelessness about the man, she thought. He was no more responsible for his behaviour than a child or an animal. He was not a rich man, but a poor one with oodles of money.

As Alice got drunker she got first sentimental and increasingly lustful as Snilesworth's primitive energy began to conjure her mixture of protectiveness and awe into something much fiercer.

The bunker, when they came to it later that evening, struck Alice as being nothing more than a rich man's den, the tree house or hidey-hole he would liked to have played in as a child.

Wrought-iron gates opened as the Mercedes drew close and light flooded the entire area as they purred towards the slab-sided monstrosity. She could sense Snilesworth's pride of ownership.

The bunker was the size of the head offices of a moderately successful company, square and hideously ugly, a parody of the finely proportioned house a hundred yards away and linked to it by a gravel path. The structure was of hard, new yellow brick which reminded Alice of an enormous public lavatory, an impression reinforced by the absence of ground-floor windows.

Closed-circuit cameras followed them through a huge steel door which swung open with a pneumatic hiss, admitting the car into a cavernous open-plan area.

A prairie of thick-pile green carpet lapped luxuriantly right up to the parking area. The smells were of new carpeting and the sterility of plastic. A small swimming pool had no smell of chlorine: the sort of people who used Snilesworth's pool would be as Snilesworth was himself – punctiliously clean.

Halfway up the wall opposite was a balcony of steel rails and glass plate. An extractor fan that had switched on automatically the second the Mercedes entered now clicked off leaving Alice to gaze around her in silence.

'It's extraordinary. It is banality taken to a new level of

refinement.' She flashed a smile, sure that Snilesworth wouldn't detect so much as a whiff of irony.

'I do my best,' he said proudly, like a schoolboy showing off his collection of birds' eggs.

'Come over here.' He put an arm around her shoulders and led her to the middle of the vast space. She was amused to see for the first time that she was taller than him. As he noticed it too, his voice became more gruff and he dropped the arm, for now they were in the presence of that which truly moved him.

A great, doughnut-shaped bank of computers stood near them. A low-pitched electronic hum came from somewhere and occasionally lights flickered. A printer rattled into staccato life, chattered for less than a minute and was still. The thing was a blasphemy, a parody of life, Alice thought, pulling her coat closer about her.

In the middle of the doughnut a sofa-sized chair ran on narrow steel rails recessed into the carpet. Some way to the left was an automatic retrieval system with robotic hands like crabs' claws to winkle items from their slots and scuttle with them to the control seat.

'This is what I'm about.' The brash confidence had returned. Snilesworth could have been six feet four.

'Sit here beside me.'

The plumpest and most over-liturgical priest could not have lowered himself into the command seat more reverentially. Alice did as she had been ordered. Snilesworth pressed a button and the chair glided away on its sinister carousel, coming to rest in front of a huge screen glowing a malevolent yellow.

'I can monitor every business detail from here, personnel records, the lot. Right down to how much paper there is in the loo.'

Alice noticed that the last remark wasn't a joke. It was a bald statement of fact. His fingers flickered expertly over the keyboard or clicked on a mouse, his white, soft hands with perfectly manicured nails.

'This area's called my command module.'

'I somehow thought it might be.'

She indicated the automatic retrieval system which had caught her attention earlier.

'Are those your books?'

'Books!' For the first time something like merriment appeared on Snilesworth's face, his smile like a slit in pound of liver. 'What would I want with them? I sacked a bloke once for bringing a book to work. All the information in the world is right here at my fingertips.'

'Information is not knowledge,' she said, knowing the distinction would escape her host. 'If those aren't book-shelves can I see what they are?'

'Printed records,' Snilesworth mumbled, apologetic for the profanity uttered in the temple of electronic technology.

'Aye, well. Some folk do business the old-fashioned way. I have to humour them.' He pressed another button and with a hum the first two ranks of racks of the retrieval system separated themselves.

'Some documents are inevitable. Deeds, copies of letters, signatures and the like. It's all old stuff. Within a year most of it will be digitally scanned.'

'I'm told you might be buying the old airfield,' Alice said, brightly as she could manage. 'That would be on paper, wouldn't it? I mean, knowing how old-fashioned the council is.' She found that she only had to mention the airfield to summon up a picture of McNally. She tried to picture him there, tall and scruffy in his leather jacket and trousers concertinaed over his boots, running a hand through his red hair in disbelief and anger.

'A lot of it is. Some of the old RAF records go back to

34

the war. Bloody stone age.' Snilesworth looked wary, like a dog fearing for its bone.

'Anyway, all part of the past now.' He tapped the computer console. 'This 'ere's the future. Why the interest?'

'Oh, I don't know. I drink there sometimes.' She felt uncomfortable under his neutral stare. He was testing her for what information she might have just as his forebears would have run the eye over a cow at market. Centuries of Snilesworths had driven hard bargains. The guileless act worked and the stare dropped. He flickered some fingers over a keyboard and a spreadsheet came up on screen.

'Wouldn't have thought it, smart woman like you. It's a dump. The new retail park will have four themed bars – Welsh, Caribbean, Beirkellar and Spanish bodega. All aimed at a target market. Watch this.'

He stroked a keypad which wafted the chair back to the main monitor and slid his hands over the keyboards. A coloured column appeared representing each of the four projected bars.

'Each one will be a little gold mine, researched down to the last detail of social class, spending patterns, expectations and aspirations. It'll be the most sophisticated exercise ever in parting customers from their money and sending them home convinced they've had a good time. It's not what they want, it's what they can be made to want that counts. Show me the youngster and I'll show you the consumer is the watchword.'

'Ignatius Loyola badly paraphrased.'

'Who?'

'A Jesuit.'

'Sounds foreign. I'm chapel myself. Anyway the kids don't want any of that. They want fun. They don't want to stand around propping up a flyblown bar all day like at that bloody old club.'

35

'One of the impressive things about you is that you have almost entirely excluded any spontaneity and humanity. Your view of the future is one conceived by the most pedestrian of minds. A veritable hymn to rootlessness and alienation.'

Perfect teeth exposed themselves in the travesty of a smile.

'Nice of you to say so, lass. I do my best.'

A plush-lined lift swished them up to what Snilesworth announced as his sleeping and dining facility. It was a vision in sterility, with all the charm and intimacy of a motel. Things like compliments, the play of words, the smell of fresh-dug earth or rain after a hot day, funny postcards, flowers, favourite jumpers and the salt-rot smell of harbour flotsam, even the smell and sound of McNally's bloody aeroplanes; ten million things which added up to humanity had been efficiently excised from Snilesworth's world. Because of that he fascinated her, just as deserts and other open spaces held her spellbound. His bunker was an expression of his being, a flat and barren plain across which she might wander for ever in search of humour or modesty.

He was different and different was sexy. Her arms went around his neck. 'I have to hand it to you. You're a complete cypher. Totally without conscience or sentiment. Quite a turn-on.'

She pulled him towards the bed and tugged at his belt and zipper. The neatly pressed slacks rucked over his polished loafers as she fished in his fresh, neatly ironed boxer shorts.

'But you do have a magnificent cock.'

Snilesworth made love industrially.

Afterwards she lay staring up through the huge glass cantilevered skylight. He lay beside Alice with barely a hair out of place and only the lightest of stubble showing. No suggestion of a snore. Even his breathing was controlled. She had expected him to shower straight away afterwards.

Alice flung the sheets aside. Slivers of ice still floated in the silver bucket which contained an unopened bottle of champagne. She ripped off the foil, fiddled with the wire and, wincing, popped the cork out with her thumbs.

Snilesworth snapped awake.

'What are you doing?' Only the slightest upturn at the end of the enquiry betrayed peevishness.

'Want some?'

She held up one of the fluted crystal glasses. Snilesworth frowned.

'Too early.'

'How did I know you'd say that?' she muttered and lit a cigarette, savouring his pained expression.

That morning she had made the decision she had been putting off for months, almost since their first encounter.

Infidelity was one thing. Infidelity involving Snilesworth was quite another. She had travelled as far as she wanted to go across the featureless prairie of his character. Time to get a bus back to civilization. She shivered, even though the bunker's temperature was electronically controlled for the benefit of the computers.

It was early, barely light. Dawn was the time when thoughts stirred, responding to the great rhythm of the awakening day. Her lust had ebbed completely. With Lawless or McNally she would have teased them awake and made them hungry for her. Lawless would have grumbled, but enfolded her in his arms, holding her tight and kissing away her infractions. No matter what he might be like later in the day with a drink under his belt he was sweet in the mornings.

McNally, the irresponsible little fool, would have been up and at it with gusto, the randy little Irish stoat, taking his innocent pleasure in great, gulping mouthfuls.

Snilesworth's punctiliousness made her feel used. She felt an urge to scramble into her clothes and make her escape. A greasy-spoon transport café lay a mile away toward Maescwm and she longed for it, cheap and cheerful and workaday: the tomato sauce crusted around the tops of plastic dispensers, rivulets of condensation streaking the windows and huge doorstep sandwiches being whisked by.

If she was going to barge into a lorry drivers' caff first thing in the morning wearing a cocktail dress and carrying an evening bag it would be a good idea to be well fortified. She lifted the glass, watching its interior light before downing it in one. The champagne raced through her bloodstream like a thoroughbred in velvet slippers.

Bright morning light streaming through the glazed ceiling and upper windows aided the euphoric rush. One more glass and she would steal away. Lawless would probably be asleep when she got home. She felt now a deep need for him.

No door lay between the bedroom and the shower. Snilesworth liked to see what he owned. The bedroom suite was the only part of the bunker that was not laid open for inspection from the balcony. Even his car was in plain view. Which is what she expected of a poor boy.

A telephone buried somewhere below in the complex tangle of wires and screens rang and was answered automatically. Snilesworth had risen and was cleaning his teeth.

'It's amazing to think everything about Maescwm airfield is here. All those people and things that have happened there reduced to a million tiny electric currents. Just the facts, though. No emotions. This place is really a mausoleum.'

She didn't care whether he responded to her sarcasm or not. He rinsed his mouth and spat. 'That's the second time you've gone on about the airfield.' His smooth and level voice slicked the invitation to a trap. A couple of minutes from waking and he was already watchful.

Impressive. Frightening.

'It's the talk of Maescwm. Members are already putting their planes up for sale not that anyone would want the clapped out old things. It's the social side people will miss.'

'It serves them right.' He swilled and spat again and turned. Alice wanted to punch him. She wished Lawless were there to knock the smug little bastard senseless.

'They could have pulled that pathetic clubhouse down years ago and built a modern airsports centre with a swish bar and a sauna to attract wealthy non-flying members. The committee should've seen the writing on the wall. Themed weekends. Corporate membership. Modern planes with a shop for fashion accessories. People want flying to be easy and comfortable, and a reflection of their status, not muffled up in draughty old deathtraps.'

'I take it from that it's all signed and sealed?'

'Sealed, yes. Not signed. Yet.'

Snilesworth carefully slotted the toothbrush into its holder. Alice momentarily wondered who cleaned the bunker and house. Robots, probably.

A second glass was making her liquor-bold although something at the back of her mind warned against pushing Snilesworth too far. He had given her nothing in their lovemaking. And for that she might have to extract a price.

Now she badly wanted to go. She lit another cigarette and blew a stream of smoke towards the massive skylight. A tiny plane was buzzing and fretting its way across the vista of glass like a trapped fly. Five-to-one McNally was at the controls, happily immersed in one of his elaborate dreams. She would go home and eat and sleep for a while and perhaps go down the club later that night to see him, say sorry for the attack with the paint spray. A battle over the airfield was brewing and in the last few minutes she'd firmly taken sides.

Already she felt like a spy working behind enemy lines. It was time to get back to her own trenches and help make the bullets.

Chapter Five

BUGGAR OF BIGGELS

Dhobi Thomas, cuddling his large gin and tonic latchlifter, otherwise known as 'elevenses', eyed BOLLOX's latest literary endeavour with a scowling mixture of bewilderment and hatred.

'Blowed if I can remember Biggles getting buggered in any of the Captain W. H. Johns stories. Never seemed the type to me,' he harrumphed.

'I don't think they mean that, Squadron Leader.' Megan pushed aside her crossword and applied herself to the explanation with the air of a professor of modern philosophy considering a fine point of logical positivism.

'They aren't making a reference to the person who habitually buggers Biggles. They mean, well, bugger off. Go away. The Biggles bit is a metaphor for the club.

'I expect they saw it on telly,' she added.

'A metaphor! I keep forgetting you're studying something trendy and completely useless at the University of Glamorgan.'

'It depends whether you call chemical engineering trendy and useless. I switched from New Directions Towards Understanding the Non-Participatory Economy last term. It was full of idle bastards like them over there.'

'Ah, a wise move. They're closet fascists. Incandescent protesters and the politically correct usually are.'

Dhobi stared into his now-empty glass as if a great truth was contained therein. 'Our great crime is to be white and overwhelmingly middle class. Wear a poppy and you're a militarist as far as they're concerned. They think flying is elitist.'

'I couldn't agree with you more, Squadron Leader. They'll never understand that beneath the booze, the extramarital sex, blustering and bullshit there are some really nice people here.'

Megan flashed a that'll-put-you-in-your-place smile and went back to polishing glasses ready for the eleven-thirty rush.

Dhobi retired to his favourite perch on the battered and sagging sofa and let his gaze wander around the clubhouse, settling eventually on the portrait of 'Joystick' Morgan, great-great-great-great grandson of the famous pirate and the club's great patron and founder.

A wistful smile flickered across Dhobi's face at the thought of what Joystick would have done to BOLLOX and to the appalling Snilesworth. Lieutenant Llewellyn Morgan had joined the Royal Engineers before the First World War and with foresight entirely untypical of him had seen potential in the Regiment's newly formed balloon section. Not for warfare, though. The powered balloons would be perfect, Joystick reasoned, for sneaking up on quail which could then be despatched with blasts from his favourite sporting piece.

Aloft one fine autumn day, Joystick had raised his Purdey to a plump pair which at the precise moment of his pulling the trigger sped behind the balloon's gas-filled envelope.

The ball of fire, which had only seconds before been the Army's prize possession, floated to earth slowly, allowing the lieutenant to escape immolation.

It had been the British military's first friendly fire aviation incident and almost dissuaded the Army Council from further experiments in the air.

'Only Morgan could be outwitted by a fucking bird,' the chief engineer was later heard to remark.

Where less-charmed mortals would have been court-martialled and thrown out of the Army, Morgan's career was barely halted, almost certainly because his parents were grossly rich.

At the outbreak of the Great War he breezed into the Royal Flying Corps, by this time with captain's pips on his sleeve, and promptly wrote off three Farnham Shorthorn training planes (which he replaced at his own expense) before being posted to a front-line squadron in France.

He excelled in the aerial duels over the trenches, attacking with verve and a complete lack of fear, once being compared to the legendary German ace, Von Richtoften.

Lord Trenchard, father of the Royal Air Force, having heard of one incident in which Morgan persistently and courageously pressed home an attack upon a squadron of British planes exclaimed, 'Morgan is a flying disaster. He's done more harm to our side than Germany's most fearsome pilot!'

In a triumphant signing-off to his combat flying career at 1300 hours on 11 November 1918, Joystick came across a patrol of German fighter aircraft making for the British lines and was among them like a hawk diving on a flock of doves, his machine guns spitting death. In his first raking pass one Fokker was surprised from behind and went down in flames, the pilot slumped over the controls. Joystick looped and rolled off the top in a screaming dive and would have rammed the next German had the pilot not decided to bale out and let his aircraft spiral downwards and end as an eruption of flame plunging into the church of a tiny French village just as the faithful were gathered to hear Mass. The third aircraft made a dash for it but Joystick downed him with a sustained burst from his machine guns all the time screaming imprecations against 'The Hun'.

It had been a fine feat of airmanship and display of combative spirit in the best traditions of the Royal Air Force. Most were agreed that had the war not ended a couple of hours before, Joystick would have been in for a Victoria Cross, or a Distinguished Flying Cross at the very least. Most, but not everybody, for Joystick was not without critics. There were those who pointed out that the German pilots were actually surrendering at the time of Joystick's deadly assault.

Had they been allowed to do so, three of Germany's topline fighters, incorporating the latest in aviation technology, would have been delivered into British hands.

Such remarks were, however, dismissed by Joystick and his supporters as mere carping.

Morgan was very well connected. Which is always useful, Dhobi reflected, when you're that bloody thick.

Anyone but Joystick would have been grounded for the rest of their career but Joystick had friends in the highest places. After one spot of leave in which he managed to blast the last 4000 breeding pairs of the rare Portreavie's ptarmigan into extinction and denude an entire Highland river system of a rare subspecies of salmon, he volunteered for flying duties in the Middle East where he won the admiration of several very senior officers.

Dhobi recalled the passage in the autobiography of Air Vice Marshal 'Albatross' Trump, KCB, DSO, DFC, who described a conversation he had overheard one day between a brigadier and a major general.

'That bloody T. E. Lawrence has stirred the wogs up properly this time,' the Brigadier had reportedly groaned. 'He's running amuck and cocking up any chance of a behind-the-scenes deal with Johnny Turk.'

'Shouldn't worry about it, old man,' the other senior officer chirruped. 'We've got old Joystick up there with a squadron of Bristol Fighters. He's bound to bomb our own side and put an end to the little poofter's capers.'

'The intrepid aviator entirely lived up to expectations,' Trump had continued, 'by pressing home an attack on a reconnaissance party commanded by Colonel Lawrence.

'Only by throwing himself from his camel was the charismatic officer able to escape the hail of bullets from Morgan's machine guns and the blast of his bombs.

'British NCOs with the column relate that Lawrence picked himself up and with a passionate expression on his face screamed at the departing aircraft, "Abuse me! Defile me! I don't care. I'll take whatever you have to give and more!"

'It is not generally known that Lawrence, after his decision to surrender his commission and join the Royal Air Force as an ordinary airman was for a time Joystick's mechanic. The pair were said to be inseparable.'

They don't make 'em like old Joystick anymore, Dhobi mused. Just as well. If they did we'd have lost World War Two, Korea, the Falklands, the Gulf and got a stuffing in Bosnia for good measure. Any country that had Joystick on its side would be hard put to sort out Luxembourg. The turning on of the runway lights in 1941 which drew the Junkers to Maescwm like a moth to a flame was Joystick's swansong as far as idiocy was concerned.

Taken away from aircraft or anything remotely dangerous or complicated he was never again able to create quite the same degree of mayhem. Still, he would give a month's ration of whiskey and soda to have Joystick involved in the impending battle with Snilesworth and BOLLOX. On their side.

Well, it wasn't going to happen. Joystick Morgan was long gone. Now in nostalgic mood Dhobi made a mental inventory of the clubhouse which for thirty years had been the epicentre of his existence. His gaze rested upon the wooden propeller presented by the RAF Association just before their premises were flogged off for a Kwiksave before shifting to the large chunk of wing complete with aileron, trailing wires and hydraulic pipes that served as a partition. Several old seats were scattered about, none of which matched. The cigarette-burned carpet, the stack of empty beer crates, the partially dismantled carburettor from a member's Yakovlev, which McNally was tinkering with, and the bent propeller, souvenir of a heavy landing, all added to the clubhouse's charm.

Soon it would all be gone and him with it. Seventy-five years of age and time-expired in service parlance.

Ten years from now at the very outside and he'd be taking orders from Commander in Chief of the Universe.

Dhobi's own RAF career had peaked with his appointment as RAF billeting and laundry officer, RAF Khormaksar, Aden, hence his nickname, a local word for laundry which had been incorporated into Service slang.

After the RAF he'd gone into teaching and done quite well until the trendies arrived in the 1960s.

His latter years in the profession had been wretched and humiliating. Passed over for promotion because he was ex-Service and therefore lacked the right 'profile' for advancement, he'd become an island around which broke waves of be-denimmed oiks with identical opinions on the military-industrial complex (against) and vegetarianism (for).

A big mistake had been to assume that such people, although perhaps misguided, stayed loyal to their beliefs, as he undoubtedly did to his. When in the early eighties left wing politics had become unfashionable he had watched with grim fascination as the pocket Trotskys slipped easily into the equally drab ranks of management.

Capitalists, having realized that most of their opponents were as power hungry as they were, had simply lured union hotshots on to 'consultative committees' where pseudo-Marxist jargon gave way to management speak without anyone being aware that it was happening.

Within six months the *Internationale* and the Red Flag had given way to the company song and the new 'classless' breed were pushing the workers around with as much relish as their masters.

Dhobi levered himself from the sofa and crossed to the window. BOLLOX was a case in point. The staff, mewling little bastards with their thin, suburban whines, had fallen for Snilesworth's scheme. He had promised BOLLOX's council bosses the money for an 'interactive facility' connected to the centre on condition that the airfield development went ahead.

The council had been nicely tucked up and too stupid to see that within two years they would not only be kicked out of bed but that Snilesworth would steal the blankets and the hot-water bottle for good measure.

Thoroughly shifty and un-British the lot of them, Dhobi thought. Maescwm Flying Club on the other hand represented the solid virtues of manliness, tradition, comradeship, honour and endeavour, even if the first of these (he thought of Hollywood) and the last (the broken-down crocks which hardly ever flew) were a bit frayed around the edges. The principles held good.

Their day would return.

When the flying club had taken over from the RAF they had discovered a World War Two-pattern flying helmet complete with intercom lead in a dispersal hut. It now hung from a peg just to the left of Joystick's portrait. A superstition was that if the helmet were ever moved from its peg flying at Maescwm would cease.

It had been undisturbed now for over thirty years. Not

even the most disorderly member had dared even to touch it. Not even Lawless in rampaging mood.

'Steady, Mr Lawless!'

Concern made Megan's voice rise an octave. Dhobi's thoughts surfaced from the cool, dark calm of the past into the troubled surf of the present.

The artist's big four-wheel-drive Jeep was slewed across two parking spaces with its door hanging open. Lawless was clutching an enormous drink which had slopped over. Glistening drops of whiskey bedewed the thick black hair on his arms.

Pink eyes attempted to fasten on Megan's breasts in a manner Dhobi thought unbecoming in a club member. He'd have a word. Unfortunately he couldn't remember the club rule which specifically forbade the ogling of a barmaid's tits, but thought 'ungentlemanly conduct' might fit the bill. He straightened his RAF tie and strode across, moustache bristling and small face flushed.

'Good morning, Mr Lawless,' in his best polite but firm voice.

'Oh, look. It's the fucking adjutant,' Lawless burst out. Burnt sienna and cadmium yellow were caked beneath Lawless's fingernails and his hair was matted and wild.

The eyes that eventually met Dhobi's slithered like raw eggs on a plate.

With an authoritative stare Dhobi sent the tittering Megan down to the far end of the bar.

'I'm looking for that randy little bastard McNally, who's been shagging my wife!' Lawless crashed a fist down on the bar and caught the rim of his drink, sending the rest of it flying.

'Mr Lawless . . . er . . . the ladies.' Dhobi held a finger to his lips and glanced down the bar.

48

'What fucking ladies?' Lawless bawled and Megan coloured, fingers tightening around a wash-rag.

'There's only Megan. A little cracker, isn't she? You
haven't succumbed to the dirty little Irish sod's charms
have you, Megan my love?'

'How personal you are, Mr Lawless!' Megan's tongue
touched her lips and her mind savoured the last tasty
encounter with McNally, while Lawless lurched from the
barstool like a bear with its bones removed. He stumbled,
grasped for the bar but lost his hold, hitting the floor with
seismic force.

Nobody heard another car stutter to a halt and the
clubroom door open and shut.

'Oh, a party! Can anyone join in?'

Hollywood held out his hands as if to embrace the scene
and then clasped them in an expression of rapture.

Dhobi Thomas groaned.

Only just past eleven and already he'd had to deal with
an emotional and crazed giant and a raving bloody poofter
with a stroppy barmaid as first reserve.

It was as if from somewhere beyond the grave Joystick
Morgan had indeed decided to take a hand.

Chapter Six

1941.

Just as it had dropped its bombs over Cardiff docks the Junkers 88 flown by Oberleutnant 'Tiger' Tschirner itself received a portion of high explosives in the form of an anti-aircraft shell in the port wing and engine.

'We should not be downhearted! Every bomb that we drop and every dock we damage makes it more difficult for the mongrel Americans to come to the aid of the English against the glorious Reich!' Tschirner bawled into the intercom.

Feldwebel Johann Lang flicked his intercom switch and addressed his superior in a tone he had been dying to adopt ever since the Luftwaffe threw them together in the same plane.

'Oberleutnant. With your permission. Fucking shut up. We missed the docks by a mile and are about to crash in the middle of Wales under which circumstances your Nazi twaddle will do us no good at all. Over.' At the time Tschirner, Lang and the third member of the crew, a beautifully spoken and shy Bavarian lad nicknamed Mutti, had no way of knowing that only one of their bombs had released.

Not only had this bomb missed the docks it had also done Cardiff City Council a favour by blowing up a notorious gentlemen's convenience which was scheduled for demolition anyway.

As the Junkers began its slow descent none of the three airmen could have guessed that they were headed towards the flying station and village of Maescwm and that Fate had arranged for them a rendezvous with Air Commodore 'Joystick' Morgan, RAF (retd) and an RAF officer who later in his career would become known as 'Dhobi'.

Although no longer a serving officer, 'Joystick' was drinking cocoa in Maescwm's control tower and offering good advice on a number of subjects to the young duty officer when he heard the droning of the Junkers' good engine and the stuttering of the duff one.

'One of ours, no doubt about it. I should get the runway lights on, pronto!' Joystick barked.

'There she is!' shouted the young man, his voice high with excitement. The Ju 88 was backlit by the red glow over faraway Cardiff. Carried away with the responsibilities of command, despite not actually having any, Joystick yanked the switch, which made the runway flare in the darkness like twin lines of diamonds set in black velvet.

'I'm not so sure, sir,' murmured the young duty officer now nervously thumbing through the aircraft recognition manual.

'It could be a Bristol Beaufighter or a Yank Marauder but it could just be . . . Surely not . . . Oh, shit.'

Tschirner lined the Junkers 88 up along the illuminated runway, the brave thought crossing his mind that he should release the bomb and wreck the place. He might have enough power to turn around again and give the hangars and huts a thorough machine-gunning before surrendering.

Self-preservation, however, suggested that if he was going to be a prisoner-of-war in about ten minutes, now might not be the time to upset the natives.

Something else was running through Tschirner's mind. Why were the 'Tommies' being so nice?

Turning on the runway lights so that any passing German bomber could blast the airfield seemed to him to be carrying sportsmanship too far, even for a people who thought that to lose at everything was the polite thing to do.

Only much later, long after he'd made a creditable three-point landing and delivered himself, his crew and his aircraft into the hands of the Third Reich's enemy did he find out what had really happened at RAF Maescwm that night.

It was organized chaos.

The moment the young duty officer identified the approaching aircraft as a Junkers 88 of the Luftwaffe he scrambled for the telephone to alert the anti-aircraft gun teams.

By the time he'd found the number of the Wrath of Grapes scrawled on the control-room wall the German plane had landed and was taxiing.

'Get your coat, man. We're going to capture some Jerries!' Joystick bawled, buckling on the Service pistol which he was not entitled to carry and commandeering a Jeep.

Jamming on his hat, the young officer clattered down the metal stairs to where Joystick was already jabbing at the car's starter button. With headlights blazing and a grating of gears they raced across the perimeter track to where the Junkers had stopped. Tschirner, Lang and Mutti were already on the tarmac with their hands up.

With the air of a landowner who has cornered a particularly larcenous bunch of peasants, Joystick strode towards the Germans with his Webley cocked. By now a motley band of mechanics and aircrew in transit had gathered to watch the fun. A sniggering leading aircraftman – for whom the sight of the ancient and pompous Joystick with the pistol holster strapped round his enormous stomach like some latter-day Falstaff and the gently weeping Mutti was too much – burst into insubordinate laughter. The young duty officer looked around nervously, desperate to fetch the RAF police with a one-ton truck.

Under the wary eye of the duty officer and with Joystick following in the Jeep, the Germans were ferried to the guardroom. Once they were locked up Joystick and the duty officer rushed back to examine their prize.

'What are they going to do now, torture us?' Mutti asked fearfully.

'Much worse, I think,' Tschirner whispered. 'They are going to give each of us a cup of English tea.'

Back on the airfield hard-standing Joystick was ecstatic, pacing around the tall, green-grey Junkers like a spaniel sniffing a retrieved pheasant.

'Dash it all, man, I shouldn't be surprised if we get a medal for capturing one of their latest kites almost intact,' and he clapped the officer on the back.

'Somehow, sir, I think not.'

'Why?'

The younger man snapped off the torch he had been shining into the Junkers' bomb-bay.

'For one thing we gave Jerry a perfect steer on the airfield. And for another, one of the bombs is still hung up. Somehow, I don't think the higher-ups are going to be particularly pleased to hear that we invited a fully armed Junkers to come and bomb the shit out of an RAF station. In fact a court martial for me and a charge of treason for you and a brief but unpleasant meeting with the hangman for us both seems the most likely outcome. Sir.'

Comprehension spread across Joystick's supremely unintelligent countenance.

'Dammit, you might have a point. Mum's the word, eh?'

'I should say so, sir. Might I suggest a good idea would be to get the plane out of sight at the back of Number Two hangar as soon as possible?'

Together they winched open the doors of the smaller of the station's two hangars. Improvising a tow-bar, the duty officer hooked it to the rear wheel of the Junkers and towed the aircraft into the cavernous gloom. Once this was done they bolted and barred the hangar.

'What about our blokes who saw all this?' Joystick asked when the furtive work was done, the edge of command in his voice by this time somewhat blunted.

'I don't think it's going to matter.' The officer's note of authority was increasing in inverse proportion to Joystick's dejection.

'The aircrews are all in transit, anyway. In a few days they'll be concerned with the real war. I'll tell them it was a top-secret security exercise. A few free pints at the Wrath of Grapes will shut the ground crews up.'

'Good show, er . . .'

'Thomas, sir.'

'Thomas. That only leaves the Jerries.'

'Oh, those,' Thomas said casually, savouring being in control.

'We'll let them go.'

'WHAAAAT? Have you gone completely mad? Let three ravening Nazis loose in central Wales? Good God, man! They'll be raping the women and rallying the Welsh nationalists and sending back sketches of the airfield to the Fatherland!'

'Have you looked at them closely, sir?'

'No. But—'

'The pilot's a bit of a politico but quite bright and must realize exactly how deeply in the pooh he would be if this ever got out. The co-pilot speaks English and seems reasonable enough and the bomb-aimer's as queer as a chocolate crankshaft and isn't going to be raping anybody. Not women, at least. As for the Fatherland, nobody there is going to give a toss about this backwater. When the choice is put to these Jerries of quietly hanging around until the war's over or being banged up in a prisoner-of-war camp I'm sure they'll see it our way.'

Fifty-four years had passed since then.

With all sorts of odds and sods of incoherent foreigners running about in the middle of a war – Poles, Free French, Czechs, Canadians, Americans and English – Maescwm had no real reason to pay attention to Tschirner, Lang and Mutti.

Indeed, in the largely Welsh-speaking village it was at first thought they were English. Many years after the war, when it was found out they were German, an anguished Deacon Prosser from the pulpit of the Bethesda chapel intoned in Welsh, 'God will forgive us our mistake. It is very difficult for decent folk to distinguish between one sort of Saxon and another.'

Joystick remained at Maescwm for twenty more years until his death, becoming life president of the flying club when it was formed after the withdrawal of the RAF.

Only once had he again set eyes on the Junkers.

Mrs Morgan had wanted a garden seat and he had dimly remembered there being a steel tubing and canvas arrangement somewhere in the aeroplane.

He had removed it himself, but after his wife's death donated it to the club where it remained in the members' bar.

Tiger Tschirner, who had flown with the German Condor Legion in the Spanish Civil War and who had been decorated by Hitler himself with the Iron Cross for 'Self-lessness in combat and stern and unbending dedication to duty and the Fatherland' now kept a flower shop on the High Street.

Lang, the reluctant National Socialist had become a fervent socialist and was chairman of, among other things, the Maescwm-Cuba Solidarity Committee and the Maescwm-Novosibirsk Twinning Sub-committee.

Mutti, the pale Bavarian boy, became an authority on orchids and a close friend of Hollywood. The two had been on several holidays to Morocco together and had once bumped into Joe Orton. Although now past seventy a certain insouciance still played about his features and he dressed nattily.

Thomas, the duty officer that fateful night, had remained in the RAF after the war and had undistinguished himself by becoming billeting and laundry officer at RAF Khormaksar, Aden.

The dispersal hut into which the Germans had been taken before being released was now McNally's home.

The Junkers 88 was still in the securely barred and bolted Hangar number two, its presence continuing undetected after some adroit administrative chicanery on the part of Thomas.

And the seat which Joystick had removed as a souvenir was the very one in which Lawless was slumped as he began to come round.

Chapter Seven

Aberdare was the furthest west Hollywood had ventured, having long ago decided that armchair travel was better than the real thing. Places never lived up to your expectations, as Aberdare had proved.

The place around which Hollywood's dreamworld turned was as far from Aberdare or Maescwm as a glittering evening at Ziegfeld's Follies was from bingo night at the local Working Men's Club and Institute.

In the voluptuous place of Hollywood's imagination, streamlined cars with glittering chrome and softly burbling 12-cylinder engines cruised perfectly manicured boulevards. Dark-haired, willow-thin women in sequin-scaled dresses writhed in tango rhythms with sinuous young men, the hot space between them heavy and sensuous as opium-smoke.

In Hollywood's Hollywood turreted mansions marbled and tipped with gleaming copper burst fantasy-Gothic from vistas carpeted with emerald grass and sweet-smelling bougainvillaea under a sky swept by magnificent royal palms.

It was as perfect, meticulous and as slightly decadent as a gold Rolex. David O. Selnick, Rita Hayworth, Orson Welles, Vivien Leigh, Deanna Durbin and Judy Garland swept into his virtual world, said and did exactly the right things with the right amount of wit and grace and breezed out again.

Maescwm it was not.

If you found interesting company in Maescwm you spun it out, savouring its preciousness. McNally, Mutti, Alice, Lawless and a handful of others at the club might not be Hollywood but at least they were Ealing Studios, a sort of Carry On-meets-St Trinians.

Everyone had to come into Hollywood's card and gift shop which meant that sooner or later he got to know their private business. When Mrs Rees bought birthday cards with pictures of trains he knew it was for her husband, who was a clerk with the Forestry Commission. If they were saucy he knew she was back on the nest with Dai the Pie. Cards inspired by Picasso, Magritte or Miró meant that Dilys the vet, who had learned bohemian ways away at college, was uselessly trying to din some culture into her bit of rough at the bus garage.

Hollywood was the eyes and ears of Maescwm and officially recognized as such by the spicy column he wrote for the *Maescwm Leveller*, founded by the radical Iolo Morgan (distant forebear of Joystick) which came out every three months – the ancient typesetting machine and clapped-out flatbed press allowing.

The *Leveller* was as much in the way of modern communications Maescwm could stand. The village tutted like a deacon at the very thought of computers, mobile telephones, fax machines, satellite dishes, cable television and fibre optics, the geegaws of the information revolution, believing that if everything could be found out about everyone at the stroke of a keypad, where was the pleasure in it?

News had to be savoured in the brown varnished back bar of the Mechanics' Arms or on the wet pavement after Chapel and there was an art to the telling. Only when the correct degree of incredulity and curiosity had been worked up were you allowed to produce it like a delinquent schoolboy unfolding his snotty handkerchief to reveal some disgusting yet fascinating prize.

When the Ordnance Survey came to Maescwm in 1838, the village had not yet been placed on any map. It had never again been able to achieve quite that degree of anonymity, but it had been outstandingly successful in avoiding the attention of the twentieth century.

A vision of the twenty-first century, involving a leisure complex with four themed bars, a five-screen cinema catering for everything from the family through to 'sophisticated adults', crèches, massage parlours, a bowling alley and Virtual Reality Mars Landing Experience plus retail outlets, a conference centre and a Handiland DIY centre was not one that Maescwm shared.

The architect of all this proposed change had never set foot in Hollywood's card shop and in all respects tried to ensure that little was known about him. This was extremely unWelsh and, in the eyes of Maescwm, tantamount to criminal conspiracy.

The day after Hollywood's unveiling of his masterplan was one of drifting drizzle, blowy enough to keep Maescwm by the side of its unseasonal fires or in the public houses. Under the dripping slate roof of the Mechanics' Arms, great business rival to the Wrath of Grapes, tweedy men attending the market quaffed pints and thumbed limp ten pound notes from grimy but full wallets.

Hollywood sat by his cheerful little hearth drinking brandy and listening to a light aircraft thrashing its way through the low cloud. Probably McNally up there fantasizing, he thought.

He carefully selected a green cocktail cigarette and lit it, letting his thoughts spiral up to meet McNally's plane. Far above the grey slate roofs of the chapels, shops and houses he flew until he could see the Regency house and its adjoining bunker.

He knew that parties were occasionally held at the house. He also knew that the only locals on the guest list were councillors and council officials, landowners and business-men whom Snilesworth wished to court. In settling back to earth he recalled his encounter of a couple of hours before when Alice Lawless had called in to buy a card.

She had chosen exactly the card he knew she would, one with an aeroplane, and had written upon it: 'To my lovely Irish bastard'. By the card display a small table had been thoughtfully provided for people to rest their cards. A cleverly angled mirror above meant Hollywood was usually able to decipher the messages.

Hers was the expected one about how sorry she was for spraying McNally's hut. He was just about to get on with some stocktaking when the idea struck that Alice's visit could be capitalized upon.

He slid from the seat and descended upon her with his just-between-us-girls chatty style turned up to maximum. 'Oh, go on. Do tell me what Snilesworth's bunker thing is like,' he started, banking on the element of surprise. 'Dreary, is it? All potted palms and nylon-tufted carpet?'

'Shag pile,' Alice said warily.

'Really! And I thought he'd built it to work in!' He screeched in his best Kenneth Williams camp laugh and slapped her forearm gently. The little routine had brought a smile and the acceptance of an offer of a cup of lapsang suchong. She'd sat where he was sitting now. Within half an hour, skilled interrogator that he was, Hollywood had pieced together a good mental picture of the vast, hangar-like bunker and of the man inhabiting it.

After Alice had gone Hollywood had poured himself a brandy, letting his plan mingle and mature in the drink's heady fumes. The whole thing would be something like Mervyn LeRoy's *Thirty Seconds Over Tokyo* made in 1944, although naturally on a somewhat smaller scale.

He had frightened himself a bit with the realization that he didn't care whether or not Snilesworth was killed in the bombing. He had never met the man and therefore had the luxury of hating him utterly. He pushed that line of thought back into the deeper, darker recesses of his mind and considered the practicalities. Snilesworth's death would end the threat to the airfield, but it would also be murder, which would mean an intense police interest in the village.

And quite apart from the threat to McNally, that would never do. Once officialdom started interesting itself in the affairs of the village there was no knowing where things would end. Shopkeepers would be brought to the brink of ruin if they were forced to keep proper VAT returns. Their customers, long used to supplementing the dole with little sidelines, would no longer have the money to spend and the whole local economy would enter into a vicious downward spiral. He tried to imagine the Wrath of Grapes, the Mechanics' Arms and the Club and Institute closing at 11 o'clock but could not encompass the full horror of it.

It painted a nightmarish picture: police cars in waiting as flying club members innocently attempted to make their way to bed, or to return home. Unthinkable, all of it. The only business to flourish under such terrible circumstances would be the post office, as the entire populace rushed to buy television licences and car tax discs.

No. It would be positively counterproductive if Snilesworth disappeared in a fine red mist. Hollywood ground out the green cigarette with the air of a man who has made an important decision and straight away lit a pale blue one.

In which case there would have to be a diversion. Snilesworth would have to be teased from the bunker before the commencement of the raid. Hollywood began to check off possibilities.

A fresh sexual lure? A nubile tidbit to tempt him forth? Megan, who might conceivably be persuaded to do her bit for the cause, sprang to mind before the idea died on the wing. Snilesworth was a wary beast ever vigilant against the possibility of compromise or blackmail.

A party, then? Maescwm Flying Club parties were memorable and invitations much sought after. But Snilesworth wasn't the type to join in profitless drinking and roistering. Anyway, Lawless would probably ruin it all by thumping the bastard and sending him home just as the bunker was being bombed.

Kidnapping was straightforward but the same objections applied as in the case of expiry.

Hollywood reined in his racing thoughts. He was getting hung up on detail. The bombing was the great, original thought around which everything else should be organized. It was like the last stanza of an elegantly conceived poem, a glorious culmination.

McNally was the perfect man to pilot the plane. The man with no official existence. One who came from nowhere and who could disappear without trace. The perfect agent of retribution.

It had to be a bombing. It had style. He dwelt on the aesthetic aspects of his plan for a few moments before picking up the phone.

A cultured foreign voice answered after several rings.

'Mutti. Hello.' The Debussy on the other end of the line was turned down as they exchanged greetings. Ten minutes later when he put the receiver down Hollywood felt giddy with adrenalin but strangely exhilarated.

Was it possible to lob a bomb through the roof of the bunker? Mutti, who had been trained by the Luftwaffe to do something not dissimilar, had said it was.

Up until now it had been between him and McNally, one of those things which are said in drink but which, by mutual consent, tail off. Now a third person was involved and the plan was taking on a momentum of its own. It would mean the commission of just about every serious crime in the book short of murder but including arson and criminal damage. It was pure drama and he stood at the centre of it, the author and director. There was no question as to who the male lead would be. Hollywood could see it already . . . the sun glinting on McNally's copper hair and on the bright aluminium of his plane, suffusing the scene with an almost supernatural quality that prefigured the dramatic climax.

And there could be no doubt about the female lead. How silly of him not to have thought about it earlier! There she would be, the older woman, torn between her passion for the dashing hero and adulation for her gifted but deranged husband, prepared to enter the bedroom of the evil genius who threatened them all!

The plan had poise and style and Mutti said it could be made to work. Hollywood could already see the credits beginning to roll.

Chapter Eight

McNally was on his way to bomb the docks at Bremerhaven when he remembered he'd left his vest drying in front of the electric fire. Bugger. It was a fine, full-fledged fantasy he was having. Now he would have to abort the mission, otherwise there was a fair chance his hut would be burned down. He checked the fuel gauge and with a shock saw it was low.

Before commencing the turn he glanced sideways to marvel at the fine lines of the other Marauder bombers in formation. In the opinion of the pilots of the 344th Bombardment Group the B-26 Marauder was the finest ship serving with the United States Army Air Force, unforgiving of fools but a loyal friend to flyers who treated her right.

Cigar-shaped streamlined bodies in natural metal finish and slim engine nacelles, perfectly sculpted engines of doom. With its advanced hydraulics and sophisticated, although sometimes troublesome, electrical system, it was the most advanced medium bomber available to any of the Allied air forces. Like a lot of thoroughbreds she had started out with a reputation for fickleness (some called her a widow-maker) and it was said that no two B-26s flew the same.

But in the hands of an experienced pilot she was superb, a bomber with the handling characteristics of a pursuit ship which could often use its 300-miles-per-hour plus to get out of trouble and with a useful rate of fire from a Bell M-6 tail turret if the pursuer persisted.

In McNally's imagination, Delwin Bentley, the cowboy-booted commander of 344th Bombardment Group and reputedly the only man who had purposely rolled a B-26 and lived to speak of it flew on his left wing.

Bentley's ship, named *Hard to Get*, with a semi-nude girl painted on the nose, fell away as McNally began his wide turn. Above and now behind, the other B-26s continued on their ghostly way. The B-26 transmuted back into a Cessna light aircraft and he was back on a heading for Maescwm.

They didn't make planes like the B-26 any more and there were precious few men like Delwin Bentley. Callous, cold-eyed, weedy, teetotal, calculating little bastards like Snilesworth were the order of the day. As the reddish square of the bunker came into sight McNally lined the plane's nose up on it and he let his imagination kick back in. He was piloting the Marauder again, listening out for the bombardier in the perspex nose.

Left . . . left . . . steady . . . bombs gone! Through the intercom and over the steady thrum of the engines.

His mind fast-forwarded fifty years as he saw Maescwm's runway now straight ahead, familiar and friendly, the most cherished few acres in his world. He gave the little Cessna half then full flap and throttled right back, watching the centre line careering towards him, flaring out and then holding off, waiting for the jolt of the main wheels touching, then letting the nosewheel down for a good landing, despite a moderate crosswind.

He taxied briskly to where another aircraft was parked in front of the big hangar and shut down the engine, sitting for a while as he often did feeling the wind rocking the aircraft slightly and enjoying the subtle and secret sounds of the stilled machine.

What he'd seen of the bunker from the air had been enough. Hollywood's madcap idea was possible. Low and slow enough, a surprise package could be lobbed through the glass roof on to the electronic devilry beneath.

'Are you nuts? You're working it out in detail.' McNally swore softly to himself and thumped the control column at the lunacy of it, but the genie was out of the lamp and seemed ill-disposed to wriggle back in. He slumped back in his seat with a resigned sigh but sat bolt upright as an acrid, singeing smell wafted faintly under his nose.

It was like the film of a Battle of Britain scramble played backwards. McNally unbuckled himself at double-quick speed, clambered out on to the tarmac and sprinted towards his hut whence came the awful pong. McNALLY YOU BASTARD was still prominent on the door, which was good, because it meant his home was still there.

The vest, which had been his favourite, nice and long, so it went under his bum and with buttons at the neck and sleeves down to the elbow was now decorated with four scorched parallel lines. Relieved that the garment had only been discoloured and not destroyed, McNally folded it and put it away in a drawer.

This simple, domestic act brought on a burst of tidying and sweeping, McNally even going so far as to run a small and inefficient vacuum cleaner over the cheap carpet and to pile dirty pans and plates in the sink.

With a cheerful pop, rumble and spurt, the antique hot water geyser erupted into life and soon clean dishes and pans were stacked high for draining. The hut had the comforting smell of old paint and wood, gas and a slight, undefinable smell of rot that reminded McNally of child-hood caravan holidays. The only household chore he never undertook was window cleaning. Every pane except one looking directly towards the clubhouse was behammocked with spiders' webs and patrolled by arachnids, who were the direct lineal descendants of the hunters who first inhabited the hut almost sixty years before. The oldest and most desiccated of the fly-corpses were already mummified when Maescwm was a wartime flying station. This appealed to McNally's sense of continuity. Five years had now passed since Dhobi, who had offered him the job, had thrown open the hut to reveal two rotting deckchairs, a rusting RAF steel-sprung bed with the pungent mattress hanging halfway on to the floor, a chest of drawers with peeling veneer and the two odd, crotchety chairs – and said, 'All this is yours.'

From somewhere above there had been a tiny scuttling in the rafters and a few grains of dust had spiralled down, suspended in such sunlight as had managed to filter through the unclean windows.

The first chore had been to beat the mattress and drag it outside for airing. That night it had smelt of crushed grass and he had been entirely happy.

During the initial cleaning he'd found a Zippo, the squared-off functional fliptop lighter used by GIs, as stylish as the automobile-like cockpit windows of the Fortress bomber or the smooth lines of US trucks and cars – at a time when British equivalents looked as though they'd been hastily assembled in a junkyard. He'd filled the Zippo with petrol and it had worked first flick. It was his single most treasured possession.

Where had the years gone? McNally had entered a charmed circle, a Shangri-la for romantics in which the normal passage of time was not only slowed but actually seemed to go backwards. Each day was a delight of flying and fixing things, occasionally fornicating and much more frequently drinking late at the clubhouse and standing stark naked at his own doorway the next morning to let the hay-scented wind clear his brain.

When Alice and Lawless had joined the club he had

gloried in the big man's utter madness and embraced his wife in a more literal sense. Being a good Catholic boy, McNally did not think it his place to refuse what God had so clearly intended for him.

With a deft flick, the last of the crumbs and fluff were expelled. He swept some change into his pocket, checked his wallet, fuelled the Zippo and left without bothering to lock up.

The walk to the clubhouse took him past BOLLOX. YOUR DAZE ARE NUMBERED FLIE BOYS was sprayed on the wall in glowing acid-green paint.

The cheerless message was underscored by Megan's long face.

'What's up?' He slapped two pounds on the bar, nodded at the Guinness pump and tried a smile.

Whatever it was, it looked bad. Seven at least on the one-to-ten scale of disasters.

The pint placed in front of him looked as depressed as the barmaid.

'Grown-up things, McNally. You won't like it. Our appeal against Snilesworth has been turned down and the wholesalers have cut off our drinks supplies. Which means that as servants of the club, you and I will soon be out of a job, fat lot you seem to care.'

'That's no way to talk to a Cwmikaze hero.'

'Don't you mean kamikaze?' Megan looked puzzled, but at least there was the wisp of a smile. With her pale, rather elongated face and finely drawn lips, she hinted forbidden and delicious things he had once known in County Cavan.

He covered her hand for several seconds.

'I do not. Kamikaze's Japanese, meaning "divine wind". They're the guys who crashed their planes full of explosives into American aircraft carriers in exchange for a guaranteed seat in paradise. Cwmikaze is the same, but Welsh.'

'"Cwm" the Welsh for valley. I see. Very clever. So you are going to fly around in circles hoping to come across an American aircraft carrier?'

'Not exactly that. But I have it in mind to save Maescwm Flying Club by the sort of selfless gesture as was made by those old Japanese fellas.' His blarney was getting him deeper into it. 'All is not lost, is what I'm saying. I think we should have a proper drink.'

Without the benefit of optics, Megan poured two monster Irish whiskies. 'Keep your money. A little token of appreciation from the club to us servants. Squadron Leader Thomas says we might just have time to booze our way through the remaining stock before the bulldozers move in.'

'How long does he reckon?'

'A month. Probably less.'

McNally followed Megan's look out the clubhouse window near to where the stump of the old guardroom stood. On the BOLLOX land opposite, a bulldozer was being taken off a low loader and parked with its blade raised menacingly towards the clubhouse.

'Bastards.'

Uttered as only one of Irish blood can, more sigh than curse, the soft sound of impending violence. Megan put the bottle in front of McNally, who poured another celestially sweet and powerful explosion, and then another.

After three more, powerful images began popping out of the bottle, flame-haired men roaring the names of old Irish gods while taking double-headed battleaxes to Viking and Norman invaders . . . Drogheda and Wexford and the cruel rape of Munster by the armies of Elizabeth I . . . the Redcoats' bloody crushing of the 1798 rebellion . . . patriots alight with righteous rage as the Black and Tans marched into their sights . . .

Another fourth belt of whiskey went the way of the others.

'Go easy. We don't want you tanked up,' came Megan's gentle reproof, her face mildly alarmed at watching the bloody pageant of Irish history march across McNally's features.

Tanked up. Words and pictures jumbling and tumbling through his brain.

Aeroplanes. With high-octane fuel.

And bombs.

He would do it. He would bloody do it for Megan and for Dhobi and even for Lawless, the crazy bugger. Even if it meant packing a plane with Semtex and in one last screaming dive adding himself to the pyre.

'Cwmikaze!'

His glass went up in a toast and Megan was now smiling brightly.

Would there be time, he wondered, for the maidens' traditional tribute for men about to go into battle?

Chapter Nine

'It's those Lawlesses again, dear.'

Mrs Frances Pugh's report trilled in her never-say-die
Guide Mistress voice was prompted by a loud crash coming
from the house next door. Cledwyn Pugh lifted his head
only slightly from the miniature lathe over which he was
hunched, and smiled distantly. The voice was the one she
had used during the war to report on the progress of
Hitler's flying bombs.

'You only have to start worrying when the engine stops.
We're tickety-boo,' was a favourite in those days.

She had last used it thirty seconds before the house came
down around their ears.

'Good old Frances,' he sighed inwardly, a picture of
poison bottles, daggers, nooses, pistols and bombs jumping
out of the locked box of his seething resentments.

He remembered that she had still been unbendingly
cheerful when they dug her from the rubble. Civil Defence
workers had told Cledwyn that it had been unusually easy
to locate his wife. 'We just heard the sound of *Land of Hope
and Glory*, guv, and followed that!'

Even in those days Frances' form was beginning to
plump out, an intimation of the vast, galleon-like woman
she was to become. Shaking the brick-dust and plaster from
her nascently corpulent form, she had given him a slap on
the back which had all but floored him and marched off to

a Red Cross committee meeting, warbling, 'Chin up! Can't let the beastly Hun see that we're downhearted!' over her shoulder.

Cledwyn skimmed the last one ten-thousandth-of-an-inch from the piston for his one-sixteenth scale model of a Pacific class locomotive and switched the lathe off.

'He's thrown that lovely ormulu clock through the French windows and now they're wrestling on the lawn. He's quite mad!'

'All artists are mad, dear,' said Cledwyn, wiping his pebble-lensed spectacles with a piece of cotton waste.

'Just as all retired teachers who are also model engineers are the very essence of propriety. Not that they necessarily want to be.'

The last sentence came softly, accompanied by a look which gazed longingly back over the years to a life that might have been, the sweet years of early manhood when all seemed possible.

Cledwyn's dreams, in miniature now, had once been on the grand scale. Cledwyn Pugh, railway engineer in the mould of Isambard Kingdom Brunel. Doctor Cledwyn Pugh, professor of English at the university in Cardiff. Against such ambitions his life should have been measured.

And what was the reality? Making model locomotives after twenty years as head of English at Maescwm Comprehensive. Life on a one-sixteenth scale.

'She's been having one of her affairs, I shouldn't wonder. It was like this the last time,' came Frances's bawled report.

'Ah, yes.' It was like the memory of some exotic dish. 'That chap with the Irish name at the flying club, wasn't it?'

It was important when Frances was addressing you to maintain the right note, somewhere between interested and deferential.

'I think it was a boy at the airfield with an Irish name. Perhaps he's still, you know . . .'

God, someone should hang the woman. She wasn't listening to a bloody word he said.

'Her husband got into a terrible paddy about that.'

'Sounds more like a terrible Paddy got into her.'

Cledwyn had a knack of speaking just below Frances's audible range. He knew it irritated her but it was his little luxury.

'I wish he'd get into you and give me a bit of peace. That's it. Why don't you get shagged speechless by some strapping proletarian with an IQ smaller than his collar size? That's if I can get anyone to straddle your elephantine girth.'

A delicious vision of squealing and kicking as a crane-driver rummaged among Frances's lower garments drove out the poison bottles and bombs.

'Do stop mumbling, Cledwyn! My God! She's squealing and grunting like a stuck pig. Do you think he's killing her? Perhaps you should go and have a word with that filthy swine of a husband.'

Cledwyn did a quick calculation on his worksheet. Lawless was 0.873 times heaver than him.

'I'm sure it's just high spirits, my love,' he cooed prudently.

Cledwyn was jealous of the Lawlesses and the passion with which they lived their lives, the masochistic luxury of their possessiveness almost as much as the panting, roaring sex.

He would have liked to have been like Lawless, larger than life, drawn to a bigger scale than other men, with passions and talents and vices to match.

'Oh my God, they're going to do it on the lawn!' Frances pressed her skirt between her thighs with the excitement.

Cledwyn blew the metal dust from a tiny file and slid the tool into its proper place in the leather wallet.

'He's thrusting his big paw down the front of her dress and— Oh, the brute! Wait. He's gone inside leaving her to collect her clothes. Now she's sitting at the garden table . . .'

The pop of a cork and cries of glee stirred Cledwyn's interest.

'Sounds like champagne.'

'So it would appear.' Frances's voice became starched with disapproval.

'After all the unspeakable things he's done to her. No doubt they'll guzzle it and then copulate without shame. It's animal.'

'It's life, my dear. Pulsating, raw and exciting.'

Cledwyn selected another file and began to apply slow, measured strokes to the metal.

Presently low moans and yelps began to issue from the Lawlesses' open bedroom window followed by the urgent thumping of a headboard.

After a time he realized that his hands had unconsciously picked up the rhythm.

Less than a mile away in the Wrath of Grapes Hollywood was in the unfamiliar position of being subjected to heavy persuasion.

'Listen to me, Hollywood. I need a bomb-aimer. You're perfect. You owe it to the club to see your idea through to its conclusion.'

'Is that what you think? Let me tell you. I'd sooner be seen wearing white socks and trainers than go up in one of your noisy, smelly little machines. You're quite, quite mad.'

Hollywood was being Noel Coward. 'Honestly. I'm surprised you asked.' To signify that he was getting bored with the subject he took a violent puff of a magenta-coloured cigarette and fixed his eyes on the far wall, arms crossed.

'You don't have to sulk. The bombing was your idea.'

Hollywood turned to fix McNally, eyes wide in wonderment at his stupidity.

'That, dear, is because I'm an ideas person. Sir Christopher Wren had the idea for St Paul's Cathedral but he didn't have to lug the stones up ladders, did he?'

Scathing. And followed up with his Kenneth Williams-circa-1964-look of scorching aloofness.

'Besides. They threw me out of the Sea Cadets because I couldn't aim a gun. What conceivable use would I be with a bomb?'

'That wasn't why you got thrown out of the Sea Cadets.'

'Oooh. Catty.'

'Look. All the bomb-aimer will have to do is lean out and throw the bomb when I tell him. I'd do it myself but for the fact I'll have my hands full.'

'That's right! Get me to do the work while you have all the fun!'

Hollywood squealed mirthfully causing heads to turn.

There must be more ways than one to skin a reluctant bomb-aimer, McNally thought. Appealing to Hollywood's sense of duty was not going to work. Appealing to his vanity might. A plan began to form in his mind.

Hollywood loved theatricality, thrived on being the centre of attention. With his last dying breath the dear old queen would probably be lighting up one of his poncey fags and regaling the company with his deliciously outrageous wit.

Right, you bugger. Watch out. There is a cunning and resourceful Irishman about.

A man standing at the bar washing down a sandwich with a pint of lager didn't realize it, but he was helping an idea to form in McNally's brain. He'd troll the bait for a while to see if Hollywood snapped.

'Do you remember the picnic after the village carnival two years ago?' McNally asked innocently, as if to change the subject.

A delay while Hollywood pondered the response, sniffing for the dead rat.

'I should do. I organized it. Or were you so drunk you don't remember?'

Indeed he did, and a fine bash it had been. People still spoke of its splendour and extravagance. There had been music and dancing and revelry on a scale Maescwm had never before witnessed. Orgiastic mountains of food and lakes of beer had been guzzled and only one condition had applied.

Hollywood had insisted that everyone come in fancy dress. No costume, no ticket, had been the only rule that glorious, riotous, randy, raucous, Bacchanalian night.

'I was a stunning Blue Angel, even if I say so myself.'

'You were that.' McNally snorted into his beer at the recollection of fifty-something Hollywood as the young Marlene Dietrich.

It was his round, but McNally scooped up their glasses and made for the bar anyway. He needed the time to think, to let the last few jigsaw pieces of the plan fall into place.

Experience had long since proved to McNally that nothing was to be lost by flinging a large gin and tonic inside Hollywood. By the time it was three-quarters down he would be sparkling. Time to jiggle the bait a bit.

'Old Dhobi is seventy-five soon, did you know? A couple of people have mentioned the possibility of a party.'

'What sort of people?' Hollywood sounded cagey.

'Just people I know. At the club. Lawless and a couple of others.'

Hollywood let out with a high yelping laugh.

'God help us if anyone of your taste organizes it! You're a complete sweetheart, but you've got no class. It'll be brown ale and stale sausage rolls!'

McNally forced a frown. 'That's just it. I told them there was no point in going on unless you were involved. You're the only person who knows how to put on a do. Dhobi is a founder member of the flying club and this has got to be a good one. Not to have you involved would be unthinkable. Would you? Say yes, Hollywood, please say yes.'

'You're an old flatterer.'

'But it's true. You're the catalyst, the man to make it happen. You're what stage conjurers make sparks and smoke with.'

'You mean I go with a "poof"?' Another falsetto peal of laughter set heads turning. McNally wondered if he would ever forget the sight of Hollywood at the party slinking around the picnic site in gold lamé slingbacks.

'It would be fancy dress, of course. We were thinking of a wartime theme. Dhobi would like that. You could be Marlene again, if you wanted.'

Hollywood looked horrified. 'My God! Think of the gossip if I came in the same costume twice! It's got to be Renate Müller in *The Private Secretary* this time.'

Hollywood sniffing at the bait, his jaws opening.

'She's along the same lines, but a bit bouncier. Not so austere and Germanic. Who could forget Renate singing "Today I felt so Happy"? Exquisite!'

'Or Amy Johnson?'

'Too butch.'

'You could play around with the part. Make it your own. Dhobi would appreciate the flying connection.'

Time to strike.

'I've got a fabulous idea for your entrance . . . Who is it you're going as?'

'Renate Müller.'

77

'Great! Be Renate Müller, and arrive by parachute! Nobody will ever have seen an entrance like it.'

Hollywood blew an agitated puff of smoke high into the ceiling.

'You're insane. It's bad enough the thought of getting in one of those death traps of yours without jumping out of it in mid-air. What d'you take me for?

'Anyway, my hair would be all over the place!'

The pause before the last sentence had been one-tenth of a second but it had been enough. The hook was in.

'Forget the plane. You'll only be in it a few moments.'

'It's the getting out of it I'm worried about.'

Reel him in. Don't let him get away.

'It will make television. BBC and Welsh Channel Four. I know a freelance television journalist who can make that happen.'

A thoughtful look crossed Hollywood's face as he patted his hair into place.

'This guy is always on the lookout for novelty footage,' McNally continued. 'Can't you see it?' He spread his hands to indicate a television screen.

'The camera is pointed towards the sky where there is a buzzing and a speck no bigger than a midge, but it grows until the viewer sees it's an aeroplane.

'Suddenly there's a roar and a blossoming of silk and you float gracefully to earth to take your bow, right in the middle of the party and in front of the cameras. Come on, can you pass on that? They'll still be talking about it fifty years from now.'

Hollywood turned in his seat, his eyes now alight.

'All right. I'll do it. Just for Dhobi. But there's one very important thing to see to.'

Please God, don't let him slip away. McNally's thin smile was inversely related to his stomach, which was sinking rapidly towards his boots.

78

'Dhobi's present. Do you think I should be carrying it as I float down in a cloud of silk?'

Hollywood's eyes were alight. He'd fallen for it!

'Ah. I'd thought about that.' McNally tried hard to conceal his glee.

'The parachute harness could make it a bit cumbersome. I've got a better idea. We could fly over the picnic and lob the present over the side. It'd be well wrapped, of course. We could practise a few times, if you liked, the sooner the better. The weather forecast for tomorrow is fine.'

But Hollywood didn't hear the last bit. In his mind's eye the cameras were turning and the spectacle of the decade was about to unfold.

Chapter Ten

A bemused Dhobi allowed himself to be persuaded that his seventy-fifth birthday should be moved forward some three months.

Club members readily agreed that a birthday party, particularly as spring turned into summer, was just the thing to lift spirits, and so Hollywood and McNally went about organizing it, apparently in tandem but in reality each working to their different agendas.

Hollywood wanted an extravagant party which would confirm him as Maescwm's pre-eminent cultural and social figure.

McNally wanted it as a cover to practise his bombing and as an undercover recruiting exercise, to sort out who was likely to be for, and who would be against an aerial attack on Snilesworth's bunker. As the day of the party approached, McNally found himself having to live a double life.

Hollywood knew that the plan to bomb the bunker was firmly set in McNally's mind but had no idea that he was being lined up as an active combatant.

Although no Maescwm Flying Club members had as yet been told anything, there was an increasing awareness, as the day for the party drew near, that something was up.

For McNally, the party would be the clincher. In front of club members he intended to demonstrate that dropping a bomb from a light aeroplane was not only feasible but offered the best chance of getting rid of Snilesworth forever.

Having agreed to be in the aircraft and make the parachute jump, Hollywood had fallen in with McNally's agenda, for now at least. Dhobi was now the man of the moment. The great panjandrum of Maescwm Flying Club had enormous organizing powers which would be vital to the plan's success.

The secretary and treasurer was, as McNally expected, at the club's bar. Apart from Megan, who had her head in a textbook, he was alone and angrier than McNally had ever seen him.

'Look at that!' Spittle flew with the vehemence of the utterance. A venomous look indicated a tall sign outside BOLLOX. It read: 'Acquired by Snapchance Developers, a subsidiary of Dreemidwell Homes for a leisure centre and retail park for Maescwm in the 21st century.'

'They've deliberately put the sign up facing us. The bastards are cock-a-hoop.'

Dhobi's normally mild blue eyes lasered hatred at the sign and the world it represented. A thin lock of sandy hair had fallen almost to his cheek which was reddened and traced with tiny, purplish veins. His lips were quivering. He was an old man, though McNally had never noticed it before.

'I'd blow them off the face of the earth, given half a chance. My God. Listen to me. The impotent rage of an old man pissing into the wind.'

Dhobi smoothed the strayed lock back into place. Resignation crept back into his lowered voice. 'I was down at the council offices yesterday trying to whip up support, but I'm afraid the man with the backhanders had been around before us.'

A grimace followed by a long swallow of whiskey spoke

distaste for councils, council officials, councillors and all other forms of government, local or national. The reason McNally liked Dhobi so much was that he was an anarchist at heart.

'The few of them who've got what might be called a conscience have been bought off by Snilesworth's promise of an extension for BOLLOX. The Tories went for the straight bribe. On balance I'd sooner have the crooks. You know where you stand.'

Megan automatically filled Dhobi's drained glass and poured McNally an Irish whiskey on the house. Ever since news of the impending closure and the drinks supplier's boycott members had been flying cases of spirit and wine back from French and Belgian airfields.

In fact, Maescwm Flying Club had not seen so much flying activity for many years. Aircraft were lurching into the air that would have looked dated in Charles Lindbergh's time.

Pilots who had clocked up the bare minimum of hours to maintain their private licences were doing that much in a couple of days as their planes rolled to a halt outside the clubhouse with crates of 'emergency supplies' on board. A siege mentality was taking over. McNally could detect a certain mood of defiance, an unfocused but discernible mood of resistance.

Which was good.

'Biggest operation since the Berlin airlift.' Dhobi's voice was lifted for a moment. 'At least we'll be going out with a bang. There'll still be a Maescwm Flying Club of sorts. The planes aren't everything.'

'Just ninety per cent!' said McNally, throwing back his drink and pushing his glass forward for another.

He needed a stiff drink before saying what he had to say. He swirled the fresh drink in his glass, pretending to study it.

'You're quite convinced about the flying days being over?'

'A foregone conclusion, old boy.'

'Ah.'

McNally took a sip of his drink and met Dhobi's cocked eyebrow. Both looked round and lowered their voices. Megan, with a barmaid's sixth sense, busied herself at the far end of the clubroom.

'Come on, McNally. Out with it. I'm the secretary. You've got something up your sleeve. You've got friends in the IRA, is that it?'

McNally laughed. If only that were true.

'I wonder. About Snilesworth, I mean. Men have been made to change their minds at the last moment, you know. I suppose what I'm saying is that everything in the world has to come to an end. But I don't see why ours should be just yet . . .' He let his words tail off.

'By Christ, you have got friends in the IRA, haven't you?' Dhobi erupted.

'I have not. But I do have something by way of a proposition for you.'

A table opposite Joystick Morgan's picture was empty. McNally steered Dhobi towards it, sitting with his own back towards the impressario of cock-ups.

'This is serious, now. How far would you go to stop Snilesworth?'

'I'd pull the trigger myself. Why not? He's out to destroy me, which is what he'll do if the club goes. I've got fifty years of myself invested in this place. It's been my friends, my memories and my life.'

As he listened to Dhobi, the whiskey began to work its fiery Celtic magic somewhere in his brain.

Suddenly the portrait of Joystick began to come alive and it was wartime Britain again. The man opposite was clearly Dhobi but now in his early twenties, fresh-faced and wearing a crumpled RAF cap. Somewhere, from another part of his subconscious, came the stutter and drone of a large aircraft, one in trouble. His mind's eye saw for a fleeting, transcendental moment the sudden flare of the runway lights, a landing and the bewildered faces of three vaguely familiar men.

It all vanished in a second, but when he looked at Joystick's portrait again he could have sworn it winked. He had an eerie sense of Dhobi having seen and heard it too. For a split-second they had each peeped through the same crack in the space-time continuum.

'You are thinking what I'm thinking,' Dhobi said softly, matter-of-factly. 'And I shall have to remind you that it is injurious to the Queen's Peace, a wanton act of arson and criminal damage which flies in the face of every law, both national and international governing the use of civil aircraft and which could be construed as an act of terrorism. If you are considering using extreme violence against Snilesworth involving aircraft belonging to this club or its members, I have to inform you that it is a bloody brilliant idea.'

McNally smiled broadly as they clinked glasses. Dhobi was in.

'I should imagine they'd be able to throw in a few other things on top of that.' He smiled and raised his glass slightly. 'Going equipped with a light aircraft and an aerial bomb for burglary, hazardous flying at night without lights and without logging my flight path, and unauthorized change of use of a building.'

'Why the last one?'

'It is an important part of my plan that Snilesworth's bunker be dramatically changed.'

'Really. What into?'

McNally leaned forward and whispered.

'A smouldering ruin. Here's to it.'

84

Members filtering in for a pre-prandial drink were warned not to disturb Dhobi and McNally. Megan kept the drinks coming and the curious away. An hour later, feeling drained but triumphant, McNally threw down the pencil he had been using to draw diagrams and make calculations.

'So you see. The chances of being caught are slim. I take off after dark with a full moon and hopefully clear-ish skies. One low pass, two at the most and bombs away! Our incendiary device crashes through the glass roof, destroys the computers and paper files and we'll be away before anyone has time to look out the window. End of bunker, end of records relating to the airfield development and end of BOLLOX's ambitions. Neat, isn't it?'

'Very. But what afterwards? What about you?'

McNally shrugged.

'I'll bury myself until the coast is clear. My strong suit is that my name doesn't appear on any computer anywhere, so as far as Her Majesty's Government is concerned, I don't exist. There will be nothing to tie me to it.'

'All right. But what if we're rumbled?'

'Spread the maximum amount of confusion and conceal any possible evidence in the way that only Maescwm can. Tell the police that a plane must have been stolen by a madman bent on his own crazed revenge. A disgruntled ex-employee, perhaps. Be cunning Celts.'

McNally stretched and yawned.

'And when the dust has settled I'll come back. Here is as good a place as anywhere not to exist.'

Dhobi's gloom of a couple of hours before was replaced by a serene, almost beatific happiness.

'You know, it's a funny thing, but people think that just because you were in the RAF during the war you spent the whole time flying about in a leather helmet shooting down Huns and talking about wizard prangs. In fact, I had a rather disappointing war. Laundry and billeting officers do. Now I've got a chance to get back at bastards like Snilesworth who have done more damage to this country than the Luftwaffe ever did.' Dhobi mulled over the delicious flavour of hot revenge.

'We're going to need some practice. Getting the height and speed right. Making sure the bomb-aimer knows when to lob his infernal device overboard, that sort of thing.'

'Which is where you come in.'

An aircraft bound for France or Belgium started up outside the clubhouse. McNally paused to listen and watch, automatically going through the cockpit checks with the pilot.

'Your unofficial seventy-fifth birthday is the cover for a rehearsal. The party will be here.' McNally produced an ordnance survey map from the inner pocket of his flying jacket and jabbed his finger on a point five miles beyond Snilesworth's house.

'On top of Mynydd Maen. You'll be guest-of-honour, of course, but your operational job will be to check how near Hollywood and I are to hitting the target. We'll overfly the bunker a couple of times by way of a reconnaissance and then head for the target area. It should be all the practice we'll need. Everyone invited to the party will be asked to help out. There is just one more thing. You'll probably see the couple of television crews on the ground. Take no notice. They're part of the plan.'

A party was forming at the bar around a pilot just arrived with a fresh continental consignment. McNally let Dhobi join the throng before quietly slipping out to the main hangar.

The next twenty minutes were spent with the dungareed figure of 'Greaser' Gordon, an ex-Fleet Air Arm petty officer, discussing the dismantling and hiding of a light aircraft following the raid. After leaving the Navy, Greaser inherited a motor repair shop from his father. Local rumour was that cars stolen in Cardiff and Swansea were recycled there, although nothing had ever been proven. Conversation was brief and to the point. McNally didn't trust the tall, dour man but he did need him.

The doubts about Greaser began the moment they parted. It could end up being a bad bit of business, but Greaser was the only qualified rigger and fitter for miles around who could have the aircraft in pieces in a trice. Better to have him inside the tent pissing out than outside it pissing in.

The responsibilities of command, new to McNally, were bringing on the most monumental thirst and sexual urge and a familiar little devil was on his shoulder telling him how to slake them both.

'Sure, if you're going to be a goody-two-shoes and fight for the underdog,' the leprechaun capered and prattled, 'you might as well have a good stiff drink and a truly momentous leg-over first. And don't we know where you can get them both?'

The club bar was cheerfully raucous and thick with smoke. Megan poured a heroic Scotch. He made a start on it before fishing for a cigarette and letting the hit of nicotine frolic with the whiskey in his bloodstream.

He smoked and drank and thought, 'If they ever found me after pulling this stunt, they'd lock me up and throw the key away.'

'Don't be daft. Your luck's runnin' good with the women and the aeroplanes,' came the leprechaun's shrill jabber.

'Get to that phone, I can see that lusty piece Alice and she's wearing nothin' except a lascivious expression!'

The drink had bushwacked the sense in his fingertips and he had to reach into his pockets to sort out a ten-pence piece.

The swelling in his trousers forced him to make for the telephone in a shambling half-crouch.

He fumbled the first coin into the telephone. Three rings and the sound of the receiver at the other end being lifted.

'Lawless here.' A deep, relaxed sonority in the voice as from a man just risen from a bed where he had slaked unimaginable appetites on an Olympian scale.

'The very man.' McNally's lips managed to utter. 'I called to invite you and Alice to a party.'

A rumble of deep mirth came back through the earpiece.

'How kind of you, McNally. I suspect, however, the whole thing will be rather tacky and unpleasant. Thank you so much, but please stick your party up your arse. Goodbye.'

'Look. It's not for me,' he managed to blurt before Lawless's handset clicked in its cradle. 'It's Dhobi's seventy-fifth and we're doing something a bit special.

'It'll go down a bomb, believe me.'

Chapter Eleven

Six crow-flown miles and 800 feet of altitude lay between the two centres of activity near Maescwm on the day of the party.

At the airfield McNally was carefully arranging large water melons around the increasingly irate form of Hollywood, who was already seated in the antique Canadian-built Beaver, an aeroplane adapted for carrying parachutists and one of the club's rare treasures. Hollywood was already strapped in and perspiring in his harness.

Several miles away, on top of Mynydd Maen, great slabs of steak, sausages, duck breast and chicken wings were laid on a table, tantalizing the buzzards wheeling in the mountain's up-currents and setting the mountain foxes sniffing. Near at hand, a large barbecue improvised from a 45-gallon oil drum cut in half was settling down to an even heat. In the lee of a large boulder an even bigger table overflowed with a forest of whiskey, brandy, gin and vodka bottles so dense that an auxiliary table had to be made from beer cartons.

Hollywood had ceded control of the barbecue and what he sniffily called 'bits of dead things' to Lawless, but had kept a tight rein on planning the 'creative' side with Mutti as his second-in-command.

Below, at the airfield, where McNally could see the smudge of smoke from the barbecue fire, Hollywood was wishing he had retained personal control of all arrangements.

'Do you think we could hurry up? I'm beginning to feel like the ingredients of a fruit salad and these things pong when they're hot.'

Hollywood was beginning to sulk.

'I might as well tell you now. If you don't get this thing off the ground within five minutes I'm getting out. I'm hot and sweaty and I can't move for melons and my costume must be an absolute fright by now!'

'Okay, we're going.'

McNally had done the checks outside the aircraft, the flying surfaces, the creep marks on the tyres, oil level and fuel and was now climbing in beside Hollywood making the plane lurch as his weight was added. He waggled the ailerons and elevator and went through the cockpit checks before forcing his hand between two huge melons and finding Hollywood's lap.

'What's this?'

'Our present for Dhobi. A silver bottle-stopper in the shape of an aeroplane. I found it in an antique shop in Brecon.'

'I would have appreciated being consulted, you know.'

There was a stutter and a roar as McNally switched the engine on, drowning further words of protest.

'Put the headphones on and don't talk until we're airborne, okay? Off we go!'

Checking to make sure the area was clear of vehicles and other aircraft, McNally made his radio calls, taxied quickly to the runway, swept round smartly on to the wide expanse of concrete and pushed the throttles forward, enjoying the rushing speed and the sense of power, and pulling the stick back until the old Beaver became unstuck.

Hollywood, he noticed, appeared to be praying.

*

On top of Mynydd Maen, towards which McNally was now flying, preparations for the feast were complete and those who had set it all out congratulated themselves with a drink apiece as they watched a brace of nuns, a matador, Frankenstein and Doctor Livingstone struggling up the mountainside towards them.

As guest of honour, Dhobi had been ferried up Mynydd Maen in Lawless's Jeep but had been spared any part in the preparations. He was sitting on a directors' chair nursing a large Scotch, praising himself for having had the foresight to put on long johns underneath his Imperial Roman toga.

Even the clear, fine weather had been choreographed into the scene. Dhobi shifted his gaze from the circling buzzards to the two distant hangars.

Using his binoculars it was easy to make out the clubhouse and the single aircraft which had just taken off and was now turning towards him.

Inside the approaching plane, McNally checked the gauges and thought how sensible he had been in asking Hollywood to turn up an hour before the intended time of take-off. It had given him the opportunity to witness an astonishing performance.

Hollywood had arrived on time, but had then disappeared into the clubhouse for forty-five minutes before finally revealing himself in all his camp glory on the clubhouse steps.

Nothing could have prepared McNally for the vision which did a half-turn and dropped a little curtsy before teetering across the tarmac to where he and the Beaver stood.

A cascade of diaphanous silk in blues and mushroom, but with hints of aubergine and purple, flowed from billowing shoulder-of-mutton sleeves past a pinched waistline to voluminous pantaloons. A brooch wrought in the shape of an aeroplane clasped the blouse and was matched by the gold pumps which peeped from beneath the bloomers.

A tight-fitting cap inspired by a flying helmet was set off by sunglasses styled like goggles. A flowing white scarf completed the stylistic nod towards an aviation theme.

Putting the parachute on had been a major task with McNally feeling more like a lackey in a star's dressing room than somebody out to rehearse aerial mayhem. After Hollywood had been placed in the aircraft and the water melons arranged around him, McNally took a moment to collect his thoughts.

There was only one thought to collect. And it was: 'What the fuck am I doing in a clapped-out old plane with a cargo of watermelons and a neurotic drag queen?'

Once it was collected, memorized, and mentally filed away as material for a biography he might one day write, McNally relaxed. There was nothing to do but go ahead with the whole lunatic plan.

There had been a bit of bother about the shoes, though. McNally had pointed out that the soft leather pumps seemed unsuited for the work of parachuting.

'Oh my God, they don't look silly, do they?' Hollywood had shrilled with mortified panic. 'I knew I should have worn silver ones to go with the blue.'

A more unwarlike figure than Hollywood was hard to imagine. His eyes were squeezed shut and his teeth bared in a wince, as though impact were imminent. Not for the first time McNally regretted not having designed and fitted a mechanical bomb release eliminating the need for a bomb-aimer.

Too late to think about that now.

'I'm flying over Snilesworth's place at a thousand feet just to get the feel of it.' McNally glanced at Hollywood, who had opened his eyes. Ahead of them the glazed roof of the bunker was about the size of a cigarette packet.

'Don't think of it as height.' He tried a reassuring tone. 'Think of it more as depth, as you would do in a boat. Being twenty feet up a ladder is much worse. Anyway it'll all be over in five minutes. I'll take her over Mynydd Maen and we'll lob out the bombs. Then you can do your party piece. The good news is I can see the outside broadcast lorries.' Hollywood craned to see the BBC vehicles and brightened visibly when he caught their toy-like shapes.

They flew over Snilesworth's bunker at under a thousand feet and not much above stalling speed. McNally's heart beat fast with the realization that a bombing attack was possible. Only average coordination of hand and eye would be needed to put a bomb right through the bunker roof. He wished now that this was the real attack. That Hollywood was clutching a genuine bomb rather than an over-ripe melon. He wanted the whole affair to be over, the waiting and planning things of the past. Leaving the bunker behind, McNally gained height. The Beaver was a high-wing monoplane and he had chosen it for its excellent downward vision. Ahead and below he could see the cluster of figures on top of the mountain.

'Now for the fun. Remember to allow for the plane's speed by chucking the melons out slightly before we reach the target. Don't hit the drinks table, for Christ's sake. We'll be nice and low and nice and slow. Good shooting!'

A sheet had been pegged down fifty yards or so from the party. McNally thought he could see Dhobi. The old bugger would be loving this. McNally throttled back and put on flaps.

'Ready with the first one.'

The mountainside rose to meet them. They would pass

over at only a couple of hundred feet. The Cessna's nose was perfectly aligned on the sheet.

McNally saw quite clearly one man toting a large shoulder-held camera and another holding a tape recorder and boom microphone.

'Steady . . . steady . . . hold it . . . NOW!'

They could almost hear the shouts as they roared overhead. McNally banked swiftly just in time to see the melon arc downwards and explode thirty feet from target.

'Not bad for a first run!' he shouted into the mike. 'Here we go again!' He pulled the plane round for another run.

'NOW!'

The second melon fell away and he saw it shatter ten feet closer than the first, a pulpy orange stain.

Elation spread across his bombardier's face.

'You're a bloody natural! Okay. Let's dump another one.'

The third melon fell within ten yards of the fire. They were getting into the swing of it. It was the sort of accuracy needed to render Snilesworth bunkerless. For the real raid the bomb would be smaller and heavier with a more predictable flight path.

He tapped Hollywood's knee and gave a thumbs-up sign and a grin before turning and coming at the target from the other side. 'AGAIN, WAIT UNTIL YOU HEAR ME AAAAAND . . . NOW!' The last package was smaller and heavier. McNally banked again and saw party-goers foolhardy enough to be standing right near the sheet scattering.

'Bullseye!'

It was Hollywood who shouted as the melon plummeted into the sheet with force enough to tear out the pegs which had secured it.

'PERFECT! NOW FOR THE GRAND FINALE!' McNally shouted into the headphone's mouthpiece. He did not want to give Hollywood time to get nervous about the jump. He climbed until the people below were barely visible, and the cars no bigger than toys.

'JUST PRETEND YOU'RE JUMPING INTO A POOL OF WATER. ONCE THE CHUTE'S OPEN YOU'LL FEEL OKAY.'

'WHAT IF IT DOESN'T?' Hollywood's voice was a terrified falsetto.

'YOU'LL STILL BE OKAY. APART FROM THE LAST INCH.'

As a joke it had the opposite effect to that which was intended.

Hollywood's face was a mask of terror under the make-up. His lips were moving but uttering no sound. It was raw, naked, knuckle-whitening panic.

'I CAN'T! I CAN'T DO IT! OH MY GOD! I DAREN'T EVEN LOOK!'

'OKAY. NO PROBLEM. LET'S GO HOME.' McNally's voice came cool through Hollywood's earphones.

'WHAT? WHAT DID YOU SAY?'

'I SAID RELAX. THERE'S NO POINT IN DOING THIS JUST FOR THE CAMERAS. WE'LL GO HOME.'

'WE'LL DO NO SUCH THING!'

McNally pulled his headset off and started a turn.

'DO YOU HEAR ME? TURN THIS PLANE AROUND THIS INSTANT' Hollywood was screaming above the plane's noise.

'AFTER ALL THE TROUBLE I'VE TAKEN WITH MY FROOOOOOOO—'

Freed of part of its load the plane bucked upwards as Hollywood's shout was whipped away by the slipstream. McNally banked and whispered a quick prayer when he saw the flare of the parachute.

Mutti, viewing the drop from below, remembered that his instructor of over fifty years before had told him that a parachute landing was like jumping off a two-metre wall.

He could not remember any trainee Luftwaffe pilot looking like this, though, making such bizarre gestures. On top of the billowing column of silk he could now make out Hollywood's face, pale despite the make-up. It seemed a very fast and uncontrolled descent.

There was a hissing, rushing sound and the sun was hidden for a second and then a thump and a yelp. Taking his hands away from his face Mutti ran across to where Hollywood was struggling out of the harness.

'Hollywood! *Liebling!* Are you all right?' He ran towards him with his arms outstretched.

'Oh, my dear, dear friend. Please tell me. Are you *kranken* – are you hurt?'

With a wince of pain, Hollywood disentangled himself from the last of the harness and fixed Mutti with a pained look.

'Hurt? I'll say I'm hurt!'

'Oh, my dear friend, I am so sorry.'

'I was waving to you all the way down and you didn't wave back once!'

Chapter Twelve

'BOMBS GONE!' McNally bawled out and whipped the plane round fast, skewering the picnic on his right wing tip.

He was elated and in the mood for fantasy. He had overdone bombers of late so decided to be the skipper of a C-47 Skytrain (Dakota to the British) coming back from a routine weapons drop to the French Resistance.

Even that didn't work and he knew why. Why fantasize when reality was so completely bloody outlandish?

Thus it was a perfectly ordinary Beaver that McNally put down at Maescwm and it was no Jeep battered and scarred by the boots and metal harnesses of aircrews but his own perfectly ordinary car that he got into after parking the plane.

Reality continued to be the order of the day as he drove up the side of Mynydd Maen to where the party was being thrown.

The metalled road straggled to an end where the Forestry Commission conifers halted like a rank of guardsmen and gave out on to bracken and tussocked grass.

A stony, rutted track tried feebly to continue the forward march of the metalled surface but after meandering upwards for a couple hundred more feet finally gave out in a green area of rabbit-nibbled grass where most of the partygoers' cars were parked.

Lawless's powerful four-wheel-drive Jeep had been able to forge right to the summit as had the BBC Land Rover parked near it.

Mr Tschirner and Mr Lang had arrived together, the former parking his antique Volkswagen Beetle next to the latter's Lada. Dhobi's carefully tended old Jaguar was there and Megan's nondescript Ford. Other cars ranged from terminally rusted bangers like McNally's to smart sports jobs belonging to the few prosperous club members.

A laugh that sounded like Alice's trilled down the mountainside. It was warm inside the old car, which reeked mustily of old leather and oil and McNally laid back in his seat and closed his eyes.

A familiar stirring came at the thought of the big thick tartan rug laid out on the soft turf with the owner of that laugh upon it. After the long and delicious sexual congress would come that sated slumber that follows sun-steeped summer days and from which one is stirred by the first breeze of evening and the earth releasing its reliquary of scents.

'Out of the question, worse luck,' McNally murmured, reminding himself of the work to be done.

'Still, if it can't be Morpheus there might be a chance for Bacchus to get a look-in later on in the festivities. And if that mad bastard Lawless gets pissed enough and nods off perhaps even a bit of the old Aphrodite.'

Laughter and the smell of cooking steaks and chops wafted down the mountain to greet McNally as he made his way to the summit of Mynydd Maen. He was enormously hungry. Although the party was in full cry the amount of food remaining was Rabelaisian. He hacked into a cheese which had been comprehensively quarried, but which was still sufficiently noble to give some idea what the spread had been like.

Hollywood had planned not so much a meal, but more a

work of art. More than a barbecue, it was only slightly less than a banquet.

From the middle of the largest of the food tables, set around by pears and peaches, grapes and pungent cheeses rose a centrepiece designed by Hollywood, depicting two nude intertwined male figures performing a *pas-de-deux*. McNally thought he had seen the figures or something very like them on the front of one of Hollywood's more dubious greetings cards.

A huge slap on the back almost made McNally regurgitate his mouthful of Stilton and apple.

'Wizard op, McNally! You and Hollywood make quite a crew.' The RAF slang and the glowing face told their usual story. Dhobi's arm was around Alice giving her the occasional squeeze.

For form's sake McNally clinked glasses and wished Dhobi a happy birthday but could not stop his eyes alighting on the outline of Alice's khaki blouse, exploring the deep cleavage, following the thin gold chain down to the pendulum which nestled in its warm and luxurious spot and mentally weighing the heavy breasts.

'Alice.' His voice went hoarse as he greeted her. 'A magnificent costume. You make the real Marlene Dietrich look like a middle-aged traffic warden, so you do.'

McNally was getting more Irish as alcohol began to thrill and tumble through his veins. By the end of the evening his tongue would be turned to silver and if another important part of him had the same sort of luck he and Alice would be tumbling in the bracken like two randy gypsies at a horse fair.

Alice shifted her American GI's cap to a jaunty angle and placed a hand on her hip to show off the waistline recently vacated by Dhobi's arm. Her tie had been slackened off completely reinforcing the air of abandonment. McNally drank in the skirt tailored snug to the hips and

99

the stockings more sheer than ever were worn by World-War-Two WACs.

'I was a bit worried about clashing with Hollywood.' There was a featherlight teasing in her smile and the whisper of delicious perversion in her almost imperceptible lisp.

'Have you seen him yet?'

'Not yet. Is he all right?'

'He's functioning. He'd appreciate a word with you, I'm sure.'

McNally didn't want to talk about Hollywood. The excitement of the flying had stirred something and the feeling was getting stronger every passing second. He wanted to throw Alice to the ground and explore the delights under the khaki blouse and her skirt, feel the smooth coolness of her thighs; then when sated, to accompany her into the territory of her dreams, dwell within the gaze of her blue eyes. He craved the spirit as well as the flesh. Of the two, though, the flesh was winning on points.

Every so often there was a chink as another bottle got thrown into the empties sack. The party was hotting up. The easy flow of chatter and laughter was all part of the easy democracy which gave Maescwm Flying Club its special character. Not a majority, but many members had served in the RAF and the service's ambience had settled on the club since its very first days, and remained a warm and comforting nostalgia.

Some members like Dhobi were retired middle-ranking officers while others had been corporals or senior aircraftmen. All, though, clung to the emotional life raft of the Mob as the RAF was affectionately known by those who had served in it.

People who had never been in the service were quite wrong to think that it bred regimentation. Exactly the opposite was true, McNally often pondered.

Individuals, loners even, took to the RAF where other services would have crushed their souls. Perhaps it was something to do with the airfields where airmen worked, immense open spaces which gave time for introspection. Aircrews functioned as a team in one sense but each member bore a full weight of individual responsibility.

Respect and affection between ground and aircrews were mutual. It was this chumminess that Maescwm Flying Club had carried over into civilian life that made the club so worth fighting for.

That and the aeroplanes – the audacious, nature-defying contrivances at the centre of it all. They were the creations of the proud and independent. They were in your blood or they were not. To love them was to soar with the big birds, content to be alone with a passion that no earth-bound person could ever understand.

It was in his blood. And although she had only ever flown as a passenger it was in Alice's as well; in the music of her make-up it was a delicious threnody in a minor key.

'Hurt or not, our star attraction seems to be dining out on his début as a parachutist.'

McNally nodded in the direction of Hollywood who, with glass aloft, was holding court amid a small group of party-goers that included Mutti.

'He hurt his arm quite badly in the landing,' Alice said, the observation carrying a definite hint of reproof.

'Being Hollywood, he has, of course, no intention of letting a little thing like that spoil his big moment.'

A BBC cameraman and reporter were in the knot of people for whom Hollywood was putting on his scintillat-ing, vivacious and thoroughly camp routine.

'How bad is "quite"?' McNally asked, alarm bells begin-ning to ring.

'Nothing broken. Sprained or something. Why?'

McNally thumped his forehead with the palm of his

101

hand. A bomb-aimer with his arm in a splint was about as much use as a one-legged striker in a penalty shoot-out.

McNally and Alice were near enough to observe Hollywood, whose eyes were lit with the telling of his story and with generous libations from a crackling good Sancerre which Mutti had thoughtfully left to cool in a mountain pool.

'Damn and double-damn,' McNally cursed audibly. His potential bomb-aimer was out of action after the very first training flight. Scratched. A line drawn through his name on the ops board before Hollywood even knew it was there in the first place.

The imp was back and grinning on his shoulder.

'Now what was it that Scotch fella said about the best-laid plans o' mice and men, McNally? My boss the Devil would've gone the whole hog and tricked yer exquisite little friend in takin' part in the actual bombin'. If you'd have put yerself into it body and soul auld Nick would have seen yer all right. If you're up to mischief then take the advice of one who knows. It's best to go the whole hog!'

'Shall we join the party?' The wholly mortal tones of Alice, still chilly, cut out the phantasmic leprechaun's giggle. She slipped her arm through his and together they strolled towards Hollywood's soirée.

The erstwhile parachutist turned from his storytelling and faced McNally with a triumphant smirk.

'It's rather put the kybosh on your little scheme, hasn't it?' This was said over the top of the glass with the suggestion of a wink and a knowing little smile.

McNally feigned innocence. Alice looked from one to the other in exasperation.

'Don't make those big round Irish eyes at me, McNally. I know what was going through your scheming little Hibernian brain. You were going to get me up there in that thing and . . .'

Hollywood clapped his hand over his mouth and came over all cute with mock-horror.

'Silly me! I've put my clumsy great foot in it again! I quite forgot that nobody is supposed to know anything about our little plan.'

Alice's look of puzzlement had been replaced with one of outright mystification.

'Know what about what plan? Will you two stop talking in code!'

She was getting crosser by the minute, a state of affairs which did not bode well for McNally's short-term ambitions. Hollywood flashed a little grimace which said 'serves you right' and turned back to his audience, who had heard and were every bit as curious as Alice.

An uneasy feeling began to grow within McNally that events were slipping out of control. At the rate the party was hotting up, it might well peak before he had the chance to make his pitch. With Hollywood out of the running his hope was that someone, suitably emboldened by vast amounts of liquor, might stagger forward and offer his services as a bomb-aimer. Upon that slender chance the plan stood or fell.

'I shouldn't despair. There's an old saying about God looking after drunkards.' The audience had gone and Hollywood allowed a note of sympathy to creep into his voice.

'One thing makes me curious, McNally. Did you really think I hadn't rumbled your little trick to get me in that plane as your bomb-aimer?'

'I thought the idea might grow on you,' McNally replied weakly.

Hollywood blew out a cloud of smoke with a laugh.

'It was rather mean of you, actually. It's a good job I can see right through you. Always could. How silly of you not to know that.'

The reproof added to McNally's glumness.

He was beginning to wish the side of Mynydd Maen would open and swallow him up.

'So what now?' Hollywood had his superior voice on him. 'The only thing left is to spill the beans about the bombing plan and hope you can find someone mad enough or pissed enough to stand in for me. Failing that, the show's over. Anyhow, since you don't intend to ask how I am you might as well go and circulate.'

Hollywood glanced in the direction of Dhobi. McNally was dismissed.

Dhobi was with Lawless who was swigging from a bottle of Spanish brandy, one immense hairy arm around Megan, whose face was flushed with laughter.

McNally cursed inwardly. Lawless was going to have Megan tonight, the bastard. That would be the bloody end, the fitting conclusion to a catastrophic day. First Hollywood had scratched himself as bomb-aimer, then Alice had given him the cold shoulder and just to put the top on it, Megan, who was to have been his fall-back position, looked like wandering off into the foggy dew with his biggest rival, the big fat spalpeen of a painter.

Some bloody evening. He was of a mind to call the leprechaun back and sign up for the whole Satanic package.

Skeins of mist were snagging in the pines above Maescwm. Many older people or those who were not dancing had put on sweaters or coats. Some of the elderly were leaving and Hollywood had finally been ordered off to the local casualty department by the village's doctor.

Only Lawless and Megan were still dancing. Alice had her knees pulled up to her chin and her coat collar turned against the chill and was regarding the dancers with indifference. McNally calculated this to be good news. Lawless was like a prize bull all tickled up and ready to cover

Megan. Which meant Plan A – the alfresco servicing of Alice – might yet swing into lubricious and unrestrained operation.

Mr Tschirner sat with the awkwardness the aged have when sitting on anything other than a proper seat. His hands were thrust deeply into the pockets of a sheepskin coat and his collar turned up against the increasing chill.

Johann Lang stirred the embers of the fire, his thoughts seemingly far away. Dhobi, his face made even more red by the fire's glow, lay with his full length facing it, his rebellious lock ruffling in the increasing breeze. Mutti the Bavarian had brought his own folding stool and was perched upon it, a couple of inches of pale yellow silk sock showing beneath the cuff of his cashmere slacks and a voluminous matching scarf insulating the neck of his three-quarter-length Loden coat.

Greaser, who had remained, sat some distance from the others. The local dentist who went by the soubriquet Gappy and his wife, a woman with unfortunate facial contours but exquisite bridgework swayed off into the darkness singing.

Greaser apart, McNally viewed the gathering with affection, Lawless grudgingly included. Dai the Pie was still nominally present, though dozing. Maescwm's bakery-shop owner had seen him through his first poverty-blighted winter with a constant supply of day-old rolls and time-expired pork pies.

McNally wished him happy dreams.

The party was now down to a small knot of people, brought together by the glowing warmth of the barbecue. All had been drinking but with the exception of Dai the Pie were not incapably drunk.

McNally's latent streak of showmanship made him hover outside the circle of light for a moment, like an actor awaiting his cue – not the kind that comes simply from the script, but the mystical pact between the actor and his audience.

A bullfight, with thousands of faces turned towards the tunnel from which the bull must emerge, was a better comparison, it suddenly occurred to him.

'I have a confession to make.'

He stepped into the fire's circle, commanding silence.

'It is not really Dhobi's birthday. The party is a front, a sham. A cover for something else. I want to stop Snilesworth shutting down the flying club and the airfield and I intend to do it by bombing his bunker. From the air. This afternoon's stunt was to have proved to you that it was possible. Hollywood was going to be my bomb-aimer but he injured himself during the drop.'

The words came out strangulated, sounding forced. He paused, weighing the silence.

'I shouldn't have lied to you. I'm sorry. I intend to go ahead with it by myself. Whichever way you cut it, an actual, physical assault on Snilesworth's headquarters is the only way to drive him away from here.'

More silence.

Not for the first time the whole idea came across as madcap, a dangerous extension of his own fantasies.

He could handle anything but this silence which made him feel like a mental patient being examined by a bunch of doctors who were shaking their heads.

It was not too late to pull out. He could say he was drunk, pass it off as an idiot remark, but the words had taken on their own momentum, pitchforking him forward. Why didn't Dhobi say something, for Christ's sake? They'd spoken about it in the clubhouse for long enough.

He was ready for howls of derision, shouts of 'Shut up, sit down and have a drink.'

He was totally unprepared for Tschirner's clipped, precise and utterly serious voice. 'As we saw, your flying is excellent and I am sure you would be able to place the bomb. But . . . your problem is that you have no bomb-aimer?'

'Correct. But it shouldn't be too difficult to rig up a mechanism . . .' Tschirner waved the rest of the sentence away.

'Bombing, you know, is not just a question of throwing something out of an aeroplane and hoping that it finds the target. It is an art as well as a science requiring precision and finesse, and at its most accomplished an almost feminine intuitive sense. But with the injury to Hollywood where will you now get this?'

'As I was about to say . . .'

Mr Tschirner smiled the smile which once meant that a factory or an arms dump or a Russian village had gone up in smoke.

'Say nothing more. I shall fly and Johann Lang can assist. Mutti will supply the necessary marksmanship.

'We of the Luftwaffe will make this bunker kaput!'

'It will be a pleasure.' Lang gave a smile which spoke of old memories. 'It is a debt we owe. When we landed at Maescwm after being hit by *fliegerkanone* . . . ack-ack . . . our friend Squadron Leader Thomas whom we honour tonight could have had us thrown into a prison camp and after the war we would have returned to a destroyed Germany. But he did not and we have had many happy years here. So, for all our Maescwm friends, we shall level Snilesworth's bunker. Professionally.'

McNally's ears were several seconds ahead of his brain. He was hearing it all right. What was difficult was the believing.

'But the aeroplane . . .' He was stammering. 'A Piper or Beaver with a crew of three?'

107

'Piper or Beaver! What is this *Amerikanische* nonsense!' Mr Tschirner snorted.

'We have a Junkers 88, Germany's finest medium-range bomber of the war, have we not?'

Chapter Thirteen

'Now *this* is an aeroplane.'

Tschirner caressed the tips of the props and reached up to smack her slender fuselage.

The Ju 88 was more creature than machine, fine-boned as a bird, arched up and standing on only a few square inches of rubber, straining to get at the sky.

Sometimes, perhaps once a year, he slipped through his secret entrance into the old sealed-off hangar, entered the belly of the Junkers and sat in his old seat, sensing the dormant life within the machine and hearing again crackling words over the intercom that had been spoken half a century before.

His flying helmet was precisely where he had thrown it after he had flown her into Maescwm on one engine only. He picked it up, feeling its stiffness where once the leather had been oiled and soft. His bald crown slipped easily into it but his jowls had ballooned over the years and he had to let the strap out to its fullest extent.

He, Lang and Mutti were doing a good thing.

Tschirner was looking forward to the attack on the bunker. He despised people like Snilesworth, those with no love of country, whose only god was gold. They were not men but ciphers, robots.

He would go through the checks one last time. Bring power to the magnetos which would in turn make the spark to flash the mighty Jumo 201 in-line engines into life. He would again feel the counterbalanced weight of the rudder, flaps and aileron through the column, recalling all these things from his memory – and the beautiful moment when she would come alive and begin to roll and then swing on to the main runway. Full power roaring and keeping her straight with the rudder pedals and back with the controls and away.

That was if the *Tommy* mechanics got it right.

He had spoken to the one they called Greaser, who had served with British naval aviation. He seemed to know what he was doing but there were no Junkers technical servicing manuals to go by.

He trusted, though, the instincts of young McNally. There was a man born with wings. He would have been proud to have had him as a son. *Ach, old man. Get out of the cockpit. It is making you sentimental.* The cowlings had been lifted from the motors. Although he still entered by his secret way the hangar had been opened and a preliminary inspection made of the aeroplane. As 'Tiger' Tschirner climbed stiffly down the aluminium ladder and dropped from behind the perspex-panelled lower blister, he could hear people coming to work on the Junkers. McNally and Lang were a part of the servicing party under Greaser's supervision. A heavy switch was thrown and spotlighting around the damaged engine came on, allowing the servicing team to peer into the complexity of pipes and wiring. The Junkers was like an old trouper at centre stage with the lights full on her and ready for her final performance.

Götterdämmerung. It would indeed be the twilight of the gods.

'What do you think, Lang?'

Lang sensed a pause where his rank would have been. Lang and Mutti had remained friends but relations between him and Tschirner retained a hint of the formality of their Luftwaffe days.

Their last reunion had ended awkwardly and the thought of it made him squirm still.

Tschirner had been drunk, recalling their last night together as an operational crew just before their motor collected ack-ack fragments.

'It must be a matter of great regret for Mutti that he bombed a gentlemen's toilet. A little like an alcoholic trying to dynamite a pub, is it not?'

Mutti had not replied and it was not until the remorse that accompanies hangovers had set in the next day that Tschirner had tried to make it up.

It was a pity, Tschirner thought, that too little had been said too late. Ah well, the other two had always stood a little apart from him, anyway. Perhaps they had been right to do so. All that crap about Aryan destiny and the greater Reich!

'What do I think about what?' Lang replied waspishly. It was too late to start liking Tschirner.

'The work on the Junkers or our chances of pulling off this . . . what would our friend Dhobi say . . . "mad stunt"?'

Lang looked up at the bottom of the port engine nacelle where the famous quartered blue and white circular badge of the Bayerische Motor Werken had been set into the cowling.

'Greaser says the motor may well be made to run. Cables and pipes have been severed but the main components are undamaged. It will be a little while before we can assess how much toll has been taken by damp and the passing years. As long as the engine has power for just a little while it makes no difference.'

'Really? I should have thought it makes a great deal if you value your skin,' Tschirner replied, suddenly aware of the old snap of authority. 'Whatever happens to us now cannot make a great deal of difference, Oberleutnant. Do you remember how you in particular wanted Germany to win the war? Well, you have lived to see your dream come true. Look at that badge on our old Junkers. Every other quality car in Britain displays it on its bonnet. What is the European Community if it is not a Fourth Reich with Germany at its heart? We have won, and even when we thought we had lost, we still had a good life. If this stunt kills us it does not matter because we only have a few years left anyway. And if we go to prison . . .' He shrugged.

'It's only where we should have been anyway.'

An ear-splitting bark ended the conversation and left Tschirner and Lang coughing in a cloud of acrid blue smoke.

Fifteen feet above them McNally's head stuck out through the plexiglass of the cockpit with a fiendishly triumphant grin.

McNally ran the engine at low revs while Greaser listened to it. Greaser signalled to cut and pushed a servicing platform back in place by the engine. McNally swung down from the blister underneath the plane, still smiling.

The last thing Johann Lang noticed as he followed Tschirner through the hangar's rusting side door was the menacing shape of a 500-kilogram bomb resting in an improvised cradle ready to be hoisted into the gaping bomb bay.

'Well?'

Lawless seemed not to hear his wife's enquiry as, teeth bared, he slashed a great streak of vermilion three-quarters the way up the canvas which then looped and plunged back to near its starting point.

Alice was draped over the battered old leather chair naked and smoking a cheroot.

'Are you going to go along with McNally's plan or not?'

The moist tip of the cheroot slid between lips glistening with the same vivid hue as the last passage on the canvas. Lawless liked the moist tenderness of young flesh but sooner or later he always came back to this, the ripe fruit. The luscious edging over into decadence. The inspired picture was going to be called *Vision in Late Summer*.

'Bugger McNally. And his simpering little poof of a friend. And the rest of the boozers caught in their time warp.'

Alice stretched and yawned, shifting so as to reveal herself fully, her crisp pubic hair with its suggestion of interior moistness pressed against the smoothed and darkened leather of the old chair.

She smiled and took a lingering pull at the cheroot. He hated her smoking. And loved it. She purred at the signs of his arousal.

'Don't get jealous. He's good in bed. But nobody can beat you when you're jealous. She blew a stream of smoke towards Lawless, who sniffed its heavy fragrance.

'Christ, you're a tart.' His voice was hoarse.

'Only for as long as you want me to be.'

'Has there been anybody since him?'

'Did I forget to mention it?' Alice said brightly and shifted her hips. 'Snilesworth.'

'I don't bloody believe you. Oh my Christ, that can't be true.' Lawless was holding his brush like a dagger, ready to plunge it through the canvas.

'Well, it is. In that bunker place of his, in incredible luxury and several times. Nothing for you to worry about, though. I don't find power and influence all that much of an aphrodisiac. Now you and McNally . . .'

'Why do you have to keep mentioning that little Irish git?'

But she could sense the theatre in this stock response and pressed on with the game – '. . . are artists. It takes a combination of finesse and authority to fly well just as it takes imagination and courage to defy fashions in painting. His control of planes and your power over paint are a real turn-on.'

Lawless's face was contorted with rage and the hand that held the brush was shaking. For a moment Alice was frightened he might plunge it into himself.

'You bloody slut. I wouldn't touch you even if I had the execrable misfortune to be McNally.'

'Oh yes you would. Come here.'

The coupling which was the climax of the game was brief and violent, the tension between them expunged by sheer physical exertion. When it was over, Alice did what she normally did, which was to put on a dressing-gown and make coffee.

'I suppose you know that an appeal against the sale and development of the airfield has been lost and that Sniles-worth can move in with the bulldozers any time he likes?' Alice looked at Lawless over the top of her cup.

'A week on Friday the place will be levelled,' she continued. 'The biggest thing left of the flying club won't be the size of a matchstick, he says.'

'I suppose he told you about it when you were in bed?' Lawless tried a snarl but the game was over.

'Irrelevant. The point is what are we going to do about it? We were there when McNally unveiled his grand plan. We didn't leave, although we could have done.'

'Alice pulled playfully at the collar of his dressing-gown and planted a kiss on his forehead.

'We're both romantics. We can't do anything else but help. I can understand you being pissed off about McNally, but doesn't Snilesworth and his kind make you shudder?'

'He made you shudder, the bastard.'

'I'm not talking about that. I believe there have to be places on the face of the earth for drifters and dreamers

114

and when you find them they become precious and worth fighting for. Old Tschirner and Lang and Mutti and Hollywood are like us. They're almost family. We come from all over the place but destiny has handed us a one-way ticket marked "Maescwm".'

'And McNally?'

'A bird of passage. He needs Maescwm and Maescwm needs him for a while. I think it will soon be time for him to take wing.'

Lawless hugged his wife.

After a while she freed an arm and stroked his beard.

'You know. It's your ability to do that which makes me love you above all else.'

'It's a funny thing. I usually feel like tearing McNally limb from limb, but his free spirit fascinates me.' Her head against his chest heard the deep, soft chuckle. 'It's almost impossible these days to live without governments and companies with computers shoving their noses into your business, but he does it. We dabble. He goes the whole hog.'

'So support him.' She kissed him again. 'Let's have a few more good years. If not Snilesworth then someone like him will win in the end, but we can buy time. We don't have so much time left, Lawless, before we are old. If the bunker is blown up Snilesworth will do his sums and clear off. I know him.'

'In the biblical sense.'

'I've admitted that. I was fascinated by the man. I wanted to get inside his head.'

'And you let him get inside your knickers instead.'

Alice sighed deeply. 'Lawless, listen to me. I happen to think that you are one of the most accomplished artists of our generation and the most generous person I have ever met, bar none. I have just been aroused and then completely satisfied by your love-making. Don't spoil everything with smart-arse remarks. And you haven't answered my question, by the way.'

'I've forgotten what it was.'

'Don't be difficult. The bombing raid. I've done my Mata Hari, glamorous spy bit. Over to you.'

Lawless shifted his gaze from the painting and smiled, a smile so mischievous it seemed to Alice that a previously undiscovered lower tier of Hell had opened upon something particularly demonic.

'We don't have much time.' Lawless pulled off his dressing-gown and stood massively naked.

'Get down to the hangar and tell McNally to count me in. There's a couple of things I need to do first.' His voice was now a stentorian roar.

'Tell him that Lawless is with him! Let slip the dogs of war! Chaos has come!'

Chapter Fourteen

They were half-an-hour crushed together in the bombard-ier's position with McNally's brain working at full stretch as Mutti carefully ran through the intricacies of the bomb sight.

He squinted down through the plexiglass and imagined fields and homes rushing by and the moment of truth when the target loomed in their sights, and the aircraft's leap as it was freed from the weight of the bomb.

Now there were only twenty-four hours to go.

When his head could take no more they went to Holly-wood's for supper and drinks, and listened to the weather forecast in silence. Hollywood flicked the switch and the voice faded.

He uncrossed his legs, leaned forward and poured three malt whiskies, large ones for himself and McNally and a small one for Mutti. The dressing-gown, the carefully cho-sen leather slippers and the way of holding his glass strongly suggested that Hollywood had decided to enter fully into the swing of things and live in his favourite 1940s film.

'Scattered cloud and a full moon. Enviable conditions,' Mutti said.

'If you're that envious you can always fly the mission yourself,' McNally shot back, nerves making him peevish.

'I'm sorry. Right up until the last moment I thought it

might be possible. But my eyes are not what they were and my reflexes . . . *ach*, are no good. You have the *schmetterling* . . . butterflies now?'

Good question. He'd psyched himself up to fly and had been suddenly deflated by Tschirner's sweeping change of plan. Being the bomb-aimer was a different responsibility. Being the pilot could be compared to being the getaway car driver. Now he was going to have to be the guy who actually blew the safe.

'A bit.'

'I know how you must be feeling. My first operational mission was on a day very much like today has been, in Russia. All the time I was looking around me, at the airfield, and then the inside of the plane and then below at the peasant cottages and the carts below, all the time thinking that these things might be the last I ever saw. When the Tommies caught us over Cardiff I was almost relieved. Did you know that?'

It must have been a lot to do with knowing that he no longer had to live a lie, McNally reflected. At least the British weren't going to throw him into a concentration camp with a pink triangle sewn on his prison suit.

'I didn't know, but I can guess it might have been so.'

'*Ja.* You bet. You know what happened to us afterwards – me, Tschirner and Lang, don't you?'

He did. When Dhobi had told him of the Junkers' landing, its concealment and the freeing of its crew it had all seemed incredible. But the living proof were going about their daily lives in Maescwm. And the Junkers. The machine had none of the neutered passivity that museum exhibits have, no matter how perfectly preserved they may be.

It was a living thing, kept whole and lethal in the aspic of history.

'Tschirner, Lang and myself owe much to Dhobi. I would

gladly do this bombing myself but my eyes are worn out and my hand shakes. I would botch it. Only you, I think, have the finesse, the sure but gentle touch.'

McNally was aware of his colour rising slightly.

'Is Mr Tschirner all right to fly?'

Mutti shrugged. 'Yes, I think so. Anyway, he says he is. This last mission is his appointment with Fate. His . . . what do you say . . . Austerlitz?'

'Waterloo.'

'Ah, yes. One of those battles.'

Take-off had been set for nine the next evening.

At that hour and time of year the bunker would be lit from within, making it the perfect target. It was rather earlier than McNally thought ideal, but after that time airfield activity would look suspicious. Before that hour Alice would have lured Snilesworth from the bunker to the adjoining house.

There was a fail-safe system. A small observation party was to be concealed near Snilesworth's house and bunker, whose job it was to ring a message on a mobile telephone back to the airfield. Only then would the Junkers be wheeled out.

At the thumbs-up signal to Tschirner high in the cockpit, the first attack by an aircraft of the Luftwaffe against a target in Britain for over half a century would commence.

'You must not worry too much. Just get on with the job. Tschirner will set the target up for you. It will be as easy as riding a bike.'

Mutti obviously thought McNally needed more reassuring.

'That doesn't help, my *schmetterlings*. The last time I was on a bike coming home from the Wrath of Grapes I came off.'

'I see that may not be a good example. All right, then. Just look at it as a job like any other. Once you are in the plane and settled down into the bomb-aimer's place your fears will fly out of the window. It will all go perfectly to plan. Tschirner, the old Prussian, will not allow it any other way. More Scotch?'

McNally put his hand over his glass.

'I'd like to but I'm bombing tomorrow. It's illegal to do it with an excess of alcohol in the blood.'

Hollywood had said little. McNally said goodnight and five minutes later was heading for Maescwm Flying Club. As he drove towards what had been the old guardroom he realized what was unfamiliar. For the first time ever no light or sound of laughter was coming from the clubhouse. He braked suddenly to avoid a hastily erected barricade.

'Halt. Who goes there?'

Alice's voice was high and female and singularly unthreatening but it made him start.

'Don't be bloody melodramatic. It's not a game.'

He was snappy with the nerves.

She wore jeans, an anorak and a bobble cap and was smiling broadly.

'Sorry, I thought you'd approve. It was Dhobi's idea to post sentries. He said it imbues us with the martial spirit. His very words.'

'Where's Dhobi now?'

Alice jerked her thumb towards the clubhouse.

'In there imbuing himself with the correct martial spirit. Blackout precautions are in operation, sir, so I must ask you to dim those headlights. Watch out, there's a BOLLOX spy about. Even the walls have ears. Dhobi is convinced that Snilesworth is using the BOLLOX people to spy on us.'

Alice pulled the gate aside allowing McNally to drive slowly forwards past a clubhouse all the more conspicuous for having been blacked out. Somebody opened the door to go to their car, sending a shaft of light across the gravel parking area.

A cocktail of natural bodily stimulants was having a whale of a party inside McNally's brain, grabbing his imagination and whirling it around in a psychiatrist's excuse-me.

In the semi-darkness the airfield and its buildings began to re-form themselves as they had been fifty years before. His mind's eye transformed the scattering of members' cars into Jeeps and little fifteen-hundredweight military trucks.

The daydream, beckoning like a ghost, led him through the steel hangar doors into the workshop areas where stood the mighty Lancaster bombers, cockpits almost twenty feet up in the air with bomb bays gaping, great pregnant creatures ready to whelp 'Hell'.

He could hear the shouts of the riggers working on the airframes and the fitters spannering and swearing beneath the engine cowls. Instrument-men and electricians were working in the cockpits and from somewhere came the sound of a radio crooning tunes of the 1940s. Armourers were stripping guns and checking turrets containing the eight Browning .303 machine guns (the aircraft's only major fault – under-armed compared with their American equivalents).

The will-o'-the-wisp dream flew, leaving the strands of reality to weave themselves back together.

The Junkers stood gaunt and warlike under the lights, a small chugging generator supplying the electrical life-force on the ground. Still elements of the dream clung. It was a 1943 version of Dhobi who spotted him and raised a hand in salute.

The plane was the focus of attention and they turned towards it. McNally's intuition was now fine-tuned and he could hear and see the recollections of a night many years before passing through Dhobi's mind.

It was easy to see it now as it had been then. The Junkers stood arched on its undercarriage struts, eager for its natural element. Hydraulic oil, compressed air and electricity were coursing through its pipes and wires like blood through the veins and arteries of a warrior.

Once again, she was a warplane, one of the best of World War Two. A Junkers 88 medium bomber of the Luftwaffe, its name immortal along with the Lancaster bomber and the Spitfire and Hurricane fighters of the RAF, American B-17 Flying Fortresses and Mustang fighters and the deadly little Messerschmitt 109s, the moth-like Heinkel 111s and the Dorniers which also carried the Black Cross.

'Are you all right?'

'Uh? Sorry, Dhobi. Just trying to remind myself I'm not seeing things. That *is* a Junkers 88, isn't it, and that's a real bomb over there. And we are going on a real bombing mission, aren't we? It all seems so bloody incredible.'

The daydream evaporated, leaving the Junkers stranded in the wrong time, a ghost come to haunt the present, deadly and menacing like a creature in a horror story.

'Greaser tested the engines and reckons the troublesome port one will be up to it. One bomb only. There'll be no going back for a second shot. Get back as quickly as you can and we'll get rid of the evidence before the police start snooping around. How are you feeling?'

'Strange. Like a man about to be hanged. Lonely. Picked out by the Fates for some loony venture which will end in tears. I don't know.' Dhobi placed a hand on McNally's sleeve. 'It's not too late. We could call it off. The aircraft could provide us with a thousand excuses.' He did not look at McNally directly. 'Do you want that?'

'Desperately. Which is why I'm not going to do it. I want this to be just like any other night and go to the clubhouse and have a sundowner and then tuck myself into my little cot, accompanied, for preference, but it can't happen. The Junkers has got some preordained connection with my fantasies and the whole tinder-box had been ignited by Hollywood's mad suggestion. I'm frightened to go ahead with it. But I'm terrified of what will happen if I back out. You don't often fly in the face of destiny and get away with it.'

The last aluminium ladder was being pulled clear of the Junkers and the generator stopped. Dhobi patted McNally's arm and without a further word turned to where the servicing equipment was already being loaded inside vans and trucks ready to be whisked away.

Greaser was standing wiping his hands on an oily rag, a baseball cap pushed to the back of his head.

'What do you think?'

'It looks fine. As long as one engine keeps going and the electrical system holds. The airframe's sound. At least it won't come unglued in the air.' Greaser pulled a cigarette from his pack, leaving a smudge of oil on its smooth white shank. He did not offer McNally one. Another little tell-tale sign of self-absorption and self-interest. Greaser couldn't help what he was any more than McNally could help what was happening to him. They were alike in some ways. Greaser the loner, yet with the love of planes. And he was a thoroughgoing professional. To get the Junkers semi-serviceable in such a short time was little short of a miracle.

Greaser puffed smoke. 'If it was a car there wouldn't be a guarantee coming with it. But it'll get you there and back. If not you can always call out the AA.'

The smile was cold and hard. As Greaser slouched off, McNally followed him with his eyes. The apprehension and excitement in the hangar was palpable, yet the man was detached. Throughout the brief conversation Greaser had not looked him in the eye. He had made a big mistake with Greaser. He'd never liked the man but now the idea of betrayal took hold. Greaser was a thief and dealing with him would taint their purpose. On the other hand nobody else could have prepared the Junkers for war. He had been forced into dining with the Devil. McNally just hoped his spoon was long enough.

People were clustered around the Junkers like a race-horse in the owner's enclosure, patting it for luck.

McNally did not want to hang around. He would nurse his own resolve until it was honed to a razor's edge.

Lang and Tschirner were talking to Dhobi, amazingly, about holidays. After tomorrow a holiday would be more or less mandatory, at least until the dust died down. He nodded his farewells to the other three and walked towards his hut.

The encounter with Greaser had somehow unsettled him. He should get some sleep. Pack first and then get his head down for a few hours. He would spend the daylight hours of tomorrow working out what was to be done with the rest of his life.

DOBEY IS A WANKER had been freshly sprayed on the BOLLOX wall.

McNally smiled grimly. If there had been another 500-pound bomb it would have been difficult to think of a more suitable target than BOLLOX.

He'd still not painted over Alice's message. No time now. The zip on the large army duffel bag was stiff with misuse until he tugged it back and forth a couple of times and gave it a dab of oil. A couple of heavy shirts, socks and pants, a favourite sweater and a book of poetry went in. James Elroy Flecker's cadences touched him deeply. A razor and cheap metal-framed mirror, his pilots' log book and his toilet bag were the last things. His valuables would fly with him, snug inside his cherished A-2. A cheap nylon wallet fairly healthily stocked with savings, his Zippo, passport and a picture of Alice encased in plastic. He planned to leave the bag hidden somewhere in the clubhouse in case the police got smartly on to the case. McNally realized that he was already accepting the likelihood of betrayal. Sleep did not come until almost dawn. Thoughts grown fantastic through feeding upon themselves grimly cavorted through his mind. In one strange and disjointed sequence he was sleeping on a tiny mountain ledge aware that the spikes that held the ropes that bound him were pulling away from the crumbling rock.

After this fitful sleep he awoke while it was still dark.

This was it now, boy, the real thing. The cold, creeping fear. Running over what had to be done with the bombsight and how the attack was to be made, checking and re-checking the details in your mind but never being able to push back the chill curtain of fear.

In one part of his dream a woman he had known many, many years before stood by the side of the perimeter track as he taxied, the blast of air from his propellers whipping at her skirt emphasizing her body's complete and deathly stillness. She was coolly regarding his imminent death. One constant thought ran through the dreams, persistent as a hangnail, or a piece of fluff in an eyelash. It should have been nothing, to be snipped off or brushed away in an instant.

But it stuck.

When referring to the Junkers, Greaser had used the impersonal 'it' rather than the 'she' used by every aviator or mechanic he had ever known.

It was the tiniest detail. Insignificant. Greaser's personal foible. Nothing as against the broader canvas of events.

Yet hadn't someone once warned him that the biggest lies were contained in the small print?

Chapter Fifteen

McNally stood. The others sat in an odd assortment of chairs garnered from all corners of the clubroom and hangar and placed in a semi-circle in front of him.

Lang and Mutti sat together facing McNally, with Tschirner to one side. Tschirner and McNally had earlier made an inspection of the aircraft and the runway.

On the one occasion it had been necessary for him to talk to Greaser he had been brief and had not smiled. Of the three Germans Tschirner had always remained slightly aloof, running even his flower shop with a crisp efficiency. People went there for the freshest flowers anywhere in the area, but not to chat.

McNally knew that Tschirner was wary of Greaser. He had not spoken of it but some subtle antenna had picked up the signals of his own mistrust. Greaser sat with his arms crossed, staring at the oil-stained canvas shoes he wore when working on the Junkers.

Lang was animated and McNally wondered whether the doctor, who was a club member, had slipped him a mild stimulant. Hollywood wore an expensive-looking claret-coloured pullover with pressed Levi jeans and clean white trainers. Lawless was sweating lightly, his shirt wide open at the neck although it was not warm. Alice was motionless and looked withdrawn.

McNally tried hard not to keep looking at Greaser but

his frequent glances did nothing either to allay or increase his suspicions. Greaser was probably a psychopath, unscrupulous and devoid of conscience. Psychopaths, he had been told, were very good actors.

Dhobi seemed on edge. They were gathered in a small crew-room to the side of the main hangar area. Dhobi was staring out of a murky window towards the clubhouse as if expecting to see a spectral Joystick Morgan flitting between the old airfield's buildings.

All were gathered. The servicing team, those whose job it was to light the runway at the end of the mission, the lookouts with mobile telephones, the aircrew and Alice.

McNally used the handle of a screwdriver as a gavel to call the meeting to order. All eyes turned towards him, the man whose finger would be on the trigger. The man who had brought to the brink of fruition possibly the wildest and most improbable act of violence against property in British legal history.

Except that this would not go down in history because there would be no trial. Not of him; not of anyone. If only he could believe that. Deeply and truly and in his heart of hearts believe it. He looked at Greaser again, almost wanting to see the face of the traitor but divining nothing. The faces in front of him were beginning to break up and change. This was not the normal, imaginative reconstruction but something unbidden and unwelcome. McNally shook his head and felt beads of perspiration forming. In a moment he would have to sit down.

The room was expanding, a haze of blue tobacco smoke suspended over seated ranks of young men. Some wore fur-lined flying jackets, others wore A-2s like his own. There was a mixture of caps and clothing and flying kit but the looks directed towards the rostrum all conveyed excitement tinged with apprehension.

He was talking but the words came from outside his own

body. His sanity had been bushwacked by events of the last few days. Now, twenty-four hours before take-off he had finally cracked. He took a pencil from his breast pocket and drove it hard into his palm. At last the faces began to pucker back into their original shapes – two, or even three times the age of the aircrews of the Mighty Eighth, who, after such briefings, had collected their heavy sheepskin flying kit, undergone further specialist briefings for pilots, navigators, co-pilots, gunners, bombardiers and finally crew briefings, before sending their B-17s or B-24 Liberators roaring away to war.

'Tomorrow night we are going to hit the offices of Dreemidwell Homes, better known as the bunker . . .' The words were coming from his own body once more. Alice was looking at him anxiously.

In the films he would have put a pointer on the precise spot on a map. As the target was only a few miles away neither maps nor pointers were necessary.

'The weather forecast is favourable with a full moon and a clear view of the target,' he pressed on.

'This is Wales!' The booming interruption came from Lawless. 'Shitty weather could close in at a moment's notice. Presumably then we'd have to abort.'

Tschirner was squinting towards the ceiling as though wrestling with an abstruse philosophical theory propounded by one of the gloomier Teutonic thinkers and appeared not to have heard.

'Not necessarily. It would be for Mr Tschirner, the captain, to decide after talking to Mr Lang and myself.'

'But what if the weather is terribly, horribly, awfully and unbelievably foul and blows the aeroplane all over the place?' The question came from Hollywood.

'I will deliver the aeroplane over the target just the same. It will merely mean a terribly, horribly, awfully, foul landing,' Tschirner said without looking over his shoulder.

Hollywood shot him a hurt look.

'That's about the strength of it. Within a couple of days the bulldozers will be here. We can't afford to postpone. Also, the longer we hold off the greater the security risks.'

For the first time his glance intercepted Greaser's.

'You bastard. You're going to do it,' he breathed inaudibly. 'And it's too late to pull back. The Devil take you.'

'He already has, ye bloody fool,' piped the little voice that these days was with him often.

McNally coughed and continued.

'The fliers are taking one sort of risk but it's no greater than that faced by the rest of you. Do this properly and Snilesworth's horrible little business goes out the window. If we cock it up the next time we meet will be in a maximum security jail. I know Dhobi wants to run through a few points. That's it. Good luck.'

'Right!'

Those who had entered a thoughtful reverie were snapped out of it by Dhobi's bark. The face of Llewellyn 'Joystick' Morgan, which cast its look of supreme idiocy across the clubhouse and out towards the hangar as if bestowing some crazed benediction on the enterprise flashed in front of McNally.

'For the love of God, don't let the spirit of old Joystick intervene in this one,' McNally muttered and was mildly reproved when Tschirner raised an eyebrow.

'At the end of the day this show is down to the chaps in the Junkers.' Dhobi lifted himself on the balls of his feet, moustache bristling. 'Which doesn't mean that the rest of us can just sit back and watch things happen. Mrs Lawless . . .' Alice, who had been worrying about McNally's mild panic attack flushed slightly at the sound of her name. '. . . has kindly offered to act as a decoy.'

Alice relaxed again, grateful she was not being asked to speak.

'She has already made arrangements to call on Mr Snilesworth tomorrow night and by 2100 hours, when the attack goes in, will have, ah . . . persuaded him to move from the bunker to the main house.

'Her and Snilesworth's arrival in the house will be the signal for the attack to commence. Timing, it hardly needs to be stressed, is of the essence. Clearly it would not be desirable for Mrs Lawless and Snilesworth to be . . . er . . . in fact . . .'

The remainder of the sentence waffled into oblivion in Dhobi's moustache.

'What you mean is the Junkers should arrive before Snilesworth has had the chance to get into my wife's knickers!' Lawless boomed, leaving Dhobi wishing he had notes to look at. He coughed instead and continued.

'As I said, the phone call will be the signal for take-off. The code word is "Cwmikaze", "Cwm" meaning valley, for those of us who don't speak Welsh, and the whole lot of course being a skit on "Kamikaze".

'The difference between Cwmikaze and Kamikaze missions is that ours come back. Or at least, we hope they do.' The joke elicited a weak smile from Lang and none at all from Tschirner.

'When the Junkers returns to base it will be up to the servicing teams to work like stink and break her down into manageable pieces. Our friend Greaser will be giving a separate briefing about that.

'At this juncture it's traditional to synchronize watches and to ask whether anyone has any questions.'

They did not. Feeling that he should set an example, McNally put his hand up. At the back of his mind was the thought that it might be a good idea to try and rattle Greaser's cage.

'Are we confident about security? Can we be one hundred per cent sure nobody's got wind of us?'

Before meeting McNally's look, Dhobi's eyes rested for a tenth of a second upon Greaser who sat with his arms folded and eyes downcast. 'He knows.' McNally said the words only just under his breath. I knew it. Dhobi is on to him. But like me he knows that the raid must go ahead. You can tell it just by looking at Greaser. Judas must have sat like that at the last supper, with arms folded and sulking. It was the posture of rejection, the first step towards betrayal. He's probably done a deal with the police; information about us in exchange for the dropping of car theft and receiving stolen goods charges. Shut up, McNally, you're getting excited. Worry about the things you can do something about, like making sure the 500-pound bomb goes right through the roof of the bunker, and stop jousting at shadows.

'No such thing as certainty in this game.' Dhobi sounded more confident than McNally felt. 'But we're a pretty tight bunch and I'm sure no leaks will come from within. BOLLOX is a problem, of course. There are more potential spies there than at Cambridge University before the war. It's also possible that Snilesworth has had men out watching us although if he has, we haven't caught wind of it. That's the best I can promise on those fronts.'

'I suppose the bomb *will* go off?' Hollywood fluted, an edge of provocation in his voice.

'Good point. Mutti? Or perhaps Mr Tschirner?'

'Of course, it has been a very long time since it was made.' Mutti spread his hands in the air. 'But I have examined it and see no reason why it should not.'

Tschirner turned in his seat to face his old bomb-aimer and in his drawn and severe expression, McNally could see another, younger man.

'The bomb was made in Germany. Of course it will go off.'

Mutti made a face and turned to Hollywood, who tittered. Bloody typical, McNally thought. Three of us on our way to commit a criminal act which would earn ten years' hard labour and all the author of the plot can do is giggle like a schoolgirl. The whole bizarre enterprise could only have been dreamed up by Maescwm Flying Club. Hazily conceived and hastily executed and terminally eccentric. Laughable, really.

Here he was with a manic-depressive artist and his nymphomaniac wife, two giggling queens, a deranged and ancient German aircrew, the former laundry and billeting officer at RAF Khormaksar and a treacherous aircraft artificer turned car-thief, about to fly on a bombing mission resurrected from more tha fifty years before.

At that moment he wanted to dash from the insanity of the room into the hangar and to find it empty of all but an innocent couple of Piper Tomahawks, a clapped-out Comanche, the Beaver, a few wheel chocks, some servicing equipment and the ancient and rusted refuelling bowser. What he did not want to see at that precise moment was a bloody great German bomber with swastikas emblazoned on its tail, its perspex cockpit newly cleaned and polished and a bomb waiting to be hoisted into its interior.

'Unless there are any more questions . . .?' Dhobi had sat down as he was winding the meeting up.

'OK. Let's get some rest. This is the last full briefing before take-off. Tomorrow night has got to seem like any other at the clubhouse although there will be more flying activity than usual. I've asked people not directly involved to fly at around dusk, which should get the BOLLOX people used to the sound of aircraft. By the time the Junkers takes off they'll be fed up listening and watching.'

As the air and ground crews drifted out, McNally reflected that flying from Maescwm was in itself a bit out of the ordinary. He'd have to make sure they didn't overdo it. Only half a dozen members regularly took to the air. The club occasionally got keen student pilots, but they tended to finish the forty hours needed to get a private pilot licence and then switch to the flying clubs at Cardiff or Swansea. Nobody took offence. Ambition and keenness wasn't Maescwm's forte, anyway. Sometimes McNally thought that if there had been a golf club near the village members would have joined that. In fact the connection with flying, tenuous although it sometimes was, would never be severed as long as the club existed. In some strange way the spell of Joystick Morgan had been cast over the place for ever. Tschirner, Lang and Mutti, although they had largely gone their separate ways over the years were bound together by their Luftwaffe experiences and what aircraft had meant to them as young men. For Dhobi the club was a link with his RAF days. Aviators and those who worked closely with aircraft whether RAF, Luftwaffe, USAAF or civilian were a brotherhood, a slightly unhinged group of people venturing into an element where, strictly speaking, man had no right to be. In general they were clubbable, extrovert, possessed of a love of mechanics and of tall stories. A cheerful bohemianism and an easy-going democracy suited them well, but there was always this sense in which they were loners.

Democracy was very important at Maescwm, for it was a Welsh flying club. It didn't matter whether a person was a poor member who had to buy flying time by the hour or one of the tiny handful with their own planes. You had to take your turn at driving the rust-streaked old Bedford refuelling truck with its cargo of Avgas fuel, painting the ground equipment and mending chocks, helping with the accounts and publicity (not much of either of those) and pitching in with the organization of social events (a great deal of that). For McNally the classless man, it was a safe retreat. A place to be taken at face value.

And where the sexual arrangements were, for the moment, convenient.

It was certainly worth living for. It might even be worth dying for. The movement was towards the clubhouse. Two members were plucked from the bar and ordered to stand sentry duty back at the hangar. They went cheerfully knowing that Megan would still be serving when they were relieved.

'I have a question.'

Lawless was receiving instruction in the use of a mobile phone. leaving Alice at the bar. She looked pale and thoughtful. They had spoken only briefly since the party.

'I didn't want to ask it in front of the others because it would have seemed silly and nothing to do with the job in hand. I just wanted to know what is going to happen to us afterwards.'

'You mean all of us?' He shrugged. 'Everything depends on how the bomb falls. If we manage to destroy Snilesworth's records completely we'll be able to carry on as we have been doing for a few more years. In the end . . .'

'Progress will catch us up?'

'Sooner or later. It always does.'

'So we're just putting off the evil day.' Her eyes scanned his face, looking for an answer.

'That's the main job in anyone's life, seems to me.'

At the bar Megan was dispensing duty-free. He supposed that if he had been a proper disciplinarian he would insist on air and ground crews moderating their intake, but Celtic fatalism was strong in his blood. If the god of war wanted to pluck him and Tschirner and Lang from the sky tomorrow they would, just as they had since man first went into combat in flying machines.

How long before the modern world caught up with them? And was their fight worth it?

The answer was in the face of the older men who stood around the bar. Dhobi, expansive and bright-eyed with gin and tonics was flirting with Megan. Tschirner, who would be the captain of the pilot on the morrow was now talking earnestly with Lawless with Lang chipping in. Hollywood was talking to Mutti, a magenta cocktail cigarette held between the straight fingers of his right hand and his right elbow supported by his other hand in his best camp stance. 'Ooooooh, do you know it reminded me of that lovely bit in the Howard Hawks film . . . what was it . . . oh yes, *Air Force* . . . where the American flyboys are standing with their Flying Supersomething stuck in the mud and all of a sudden these gorgeous RAF boys come running out and get it out for them . . .'

Hollywood had given himself over to being the mission's joker. It was good to have the frivolous touch. To remind them that nothing, in the end, was to be taken too seriously.

Long enough for Dhobi and Tschirner and Lang and Mutti, and perhaps even Hollywood, to live out the rest of their lives. Most of the club was middle-aged or downright old. When they died the club would die with them. Fifteen years at the very outside. Then Snilesworth or someone very much like him would have their way.

The notion of progress had always eluded McNally, who often thought that the only useful thing invented since about 1938 had been relatively painless dental surgery. All the things that had the potential to make people's lives more fulfilling or comfortable were in existence by that time. Of the inventions that had come later two stood out as supremely evil. Television had sucked people's brains dry of imagination, that most precious crucible where compassion and art were forged. Computers had taken away work from hands and minds leaving a discontented and demoralized population, whose only consolation was in acquiring things. Television then closed this terrible circle by telling them of the things they should acquire. One man in a thousand a genuine hero, broke the circle.

Was he, he wondered, the stuff of heroes? Probably not. Most men who performed well in battle did so because they were frightened or angry, or even bored. He was angry and the thought of Snilesworth fed the flickering light of his wrath. Snilesworth was more than a thief of land and money, more than merely a trickster and a fraud on the material level. He stole men's dreams. Disturbed the little worlds they had created for themselves and replaced them with his own form of bloodless conformity. That's why his bunker would, God willing, soon be a smoking shell.

'I wouldn't worry too much if the little bastard is inside when our 500-poundsworth of revenge goes shattering through his skylight.'

'That's me boy, McNally,' said the little imp who had skipped back on his shoulder.

'You don't mean that. You're not that ruthless,' said Alice who, in a swift, darting motion, stroked his cheek, a brush so light he could have dreamt it.

'It's just the Irish in you and it's written all over your lovely face, those blue eyes with their hungry look and those ginger curls. You'd kill in anger or in drink but not in cold blood.'

'And Snilesworth would?'

'He might.' She glanced towards where Lawless was still talking, making sure their talk was still private.

'All that electronic wizardry in his bunker is a way of distancing himself from the pain he causes. He evicts people, or ruins their lives at the push of a button. I don't know whether it gives him pleasure. It probably does, because people like him are hooked on efficiency. You, McNally, might easily kill somebody in a rage. He's too controlled. The essence of his life is in the reining in of emotion, including compassion. You'd be a bloody hope-less capitalist.'

Jealousy tweaked him with its delicious pain.

'You know about him because you've slept with him.'

It was said bitterly. Alice coloured.

'You're so right.' Her lips pressed into a thin, hard line, her stare level and cold. 'And if the attack on the bunker is to succeed I'll probably have to sleep with him again. Does that make you jealous?'

'You know it does. Lawless I can handle. I like him in a funny sort of way. The thought of you with Snilesworth turns my stomach.'

'You're a self-centred little sod, aren't you?'

In that moment McNally saw her pure, glittering anger and was afraid. Imperceptibly he moved back like a hound retreating from a cornered cat, but she shifted her body forward, conscious of having won ground and now wishing to press home the advantage.

He realized what should have been blindingly obvious. He'd been a fool not to see it. His part in the bombing was no longer the most important. He would squint down the Lofte tachometric bombsight that Mutti had familiarized him with and let the bomb go. His job was to be a mere extension of the Junkers.

The real battle would be waged inside the bunker and the house. Whatever Alice needed to do to transfer Snilesworth from the bunker to the house she would do. She would commit all to the fight.

It was upon her as much as himself, Tschirner and Lang that the forthcoming battle turned.

'Even if there was another way out of this, it's too late.' His voice was strained.

'I know. So let's get on with it.'

He offered her another drink which was refused politely, her anger on the ebb.

'I think I should spend some time with Lawless. It's not exactly a picnic for him.'

'I do know that. I'm not completely insensitive.'

137

Her smile had a wisp of forgiveness as she turned away.

McNally had another drink, a small one this time before walking to his hut which was now bare apart from the bedding and his washing kit. Even that would be spirited away within the next few hours.

He lay down, trying to think of the men who had occupied the hut during the Second World War but feeling only a hollowness. This is how it had been for them, he thought. Hating the planes which would take them to a possible death, ridiculing the medals and uniforms. Praying for it to be over. Feeling like condemned men waiting for the tread of the prison governor and his retinue to usher them into eternity.

He wondered what Tschirner and Lang were thinking at that moment. After half an hour sleep drew itself over his exhausted mind like a threadbare blanket.

Chapter Sixteen

It was a fine day for the first bombing run by a Junkers 88 since the end of the Second World War.

The sad, pale luminescence of dawn had yielded a warm sun which was now warming the faded paint of McNally's old dispersal hut and vigorously sucking the last pearl of dew from the flying field's untamed grass. McNally lay on his army cot listening to his hut creaking and drying and sighing like an old man warming his bones.

After a few minutes he got up, retrieved his kettle and a tin mug where he had set them in a corner and set to making tea.

For ten minutes with the tea and a cigarette he sat in the tattered folding chair, looking towards the main hangar.

Already the sun was causing the shimmering of heat-haze over the perimeter track. Only the very slightest breeze wafted the feathery ears of the grass.

He smoked the cigarette and immediately lighted another, the first one for the nicotine, the second as a kind of ritual leave-taking, symbolic of all the cigarettes he had ever smoked in the hut.

A cricket chirruped nearby.

As soon as the last of the night's moisture was evaporated insects would commence their buzzing overture, a hundred thousand little miracles of flight all around him. He remembered the half-bottle of whiskey in the glove compartment of his car and rose to fetch it, slurping a generous amount in his tea. He walked barefoot, feeling the grass still cool underfoot before settling back in the old chair.

Drinking and flying was against all the rules but so was blowing somebody's offices to hell.

In a peculiar way McNally felt at peace with the world. It was like being at the eye of a storm. Kamikaze pilots must have felt like it, he reflected, in the hours before they climbed into their stripped-down Zero fighters, made a final salute to the God-Emperor and gave a Banzai, slammed shut their cockpits' hoods and fired up their engines for a last flight into oblivion.

What had to be done had to be done and only an act of God could now call events to a halt. Since hardly anyone lifted a finger in Maescwm it seemed unlikely that the Almighty would now go too far out of his way.

Prayer bells tinkling in the wind, whispering paper streamers making their modest contributions to God's peace, that's what the young fliers soon to be borne on the Divine Wind would have wished to hear on a morning like this one. '. . . I GOT RABIES AN I WANNA BITE YOUR BABEEES . . . I GOT RABIES AN I WANNA BITE YOUR BABEEES . . . I GOT RABIES AN I WANNA BITE EM NAAAAAAAAAAAA . . .'

The sudden blast of noise emanating from BOLLOX seemed to bend the very grass stalks with its crashing discordance.

McNally jerked upright, his heart racing, adrenalin pulsing out the instinctive signal, 'fight or flight'. The sound carried on for a few bars more and then stopped with a screech of overpowered speakers. It was several moments before the scar in the silence was healed, by which time McNally was on his feet, his face flushed. He threw down his cigarette angrily and ground it out forgetting he was barefoot.

He yelped, swore at BOLLOX in particular and Fate in general and hopped inside the hut to dress. He composed himself with the ritual of washing at his small ceramic sink. Having scrubbed his teeth he rinsed the brush and, together with the toothpaste, placed it in his toilet bag which he replaced in his zipper bag.

He washed carefully, first his face and hands and then wincing as he slapped the cold facecloth over his private parts.

He debated whether to shave and decided that to drag a cold razor over his face would be marginally less painful than having to face Tschirner's reproving look. Today he would be flying as aircrew in the Junkers 88, the best medium bomber ever designed for the Luftwaffe and one of the classic aeroplanes of the war. Such an event deserved a reasonably presentable appearance.

After his ordeal with the razor McNally eyed the malignant instrument for a second and vowed one day to grow a beard. After stowing it with the other toiletries, he flicked a comb through his hair, dropped the snib, and shut the door and drove towards the clubhouse without looking back.

Dhobi was inside, fortifying himself against the rigours of the day to come with his first drink, what he called his latchlifter. McNally placed the key to his hut on the table and flung his bag behind the bar.

It struck him that he was now homeless and free of the material possessions that connected a man to the world. If it all went terminally wrong he would be facing Death pretty much as he had faced the first moment of life.

'Busy morning, old boy. Quite like the old days. Excitement in the air and all that.' Dhobi beamed.

Not the sort of thing that could normally be said about

Maescwm with any degree of accuracy, but this morning quite true. Sleepy haphazardness had been dispelled by hive-like activity.

'Almost military, isn't it? Chaps busy everywhere. Chapesses as well.' It did indeed remind McNally of his air force days. There was a purposefulness about people very much like that of ground crews on a flying station who possessed a deceptively casual attitude towards the complex monsters with which they were entrusted.

Both were at first reluctant to mention the coming night's business. McNally left it to Dhobi to broach the subject.

'Weather's good for tonight. I asked Tschirner if he wanted to take the little Piper Tomahawk up for a last recce. Get his eye in. He didn't want to. He was a bit off with me, actually. She's there if you want to take her up.'

'That's all right.'

He didn't want to climb into the tiny cockpit, prime the carb and send her skipping down the runway with a nice light lift-off at around seventy miles an hour. The tough, lovely little Piper with its pert, high tail belonged to another, carefree time. His business now was with Junkers and bombsights.

He tried to move his thoughts on, past the raid. There was no telling now when he might be at the controls of an aircraft again. Unable to probe the mists of the future he forced himself back into the present.

'It'll spoil my luck. Tschirner and Lang know what they're doing. What's the news on the Junkers?'

Dhobi raised his eyebrows and pursed his lips. 'Not my department, really, but I think Greaser's prepared to put his name on the RAF form 700 to say she's okay. The engines are running up well.'

'The bomb release mechanism is what concerns me. God forbid that the bomb hangs up and we remove some unsuspecting little hamlet from the map. I'm going to make a last check.'

'Relax, McNally. Come on. One last pre-op drink with me?'

Dhobi helped McNally to a small Scotch and himself to a large gin and tonic.

As they drank a member rushed in, leaving the door gaping, snatched up the Junkers 88 access panel which had been repaired by a local sheet metal worker, tapped it and felt the alignment of the rivets and slammed the door behind him, leaving them alone once more.

'What will you do after tonight?'

Dhobi stared into his glass, rotated the contents and swallowed.

Cue answer for a question he had many times asked himself.

'Dunno. Hide. Go abroad for a bit and come back when the coast is clear. They're bound to tie me in with it eventually. People talk, especially here in Wales. Perhaps after a couple of years I'll be able to grow a big beard and acquire a new name and take up where I left off. It's the nearest I've got to a plan.'

The old Bedford fuel bowser rasped into life from somewhere outside. They were fuelling the Junkers. McNally knew the club's kitty had been cleaned out to pay for the aviation gasoline.

Everything was being risked on one roll of the dice, or rather one drop of the bomb.

Only rarely over the last five years had the Maescwm Flying Club managed to collect enough money to be able to fill the tanker with Avgas. A joke was that cards issued to new members should bear the wording: 'Members are advised to bring their own fuel in a tightly sealed and approved container.'

The other half of the joke was that there had been no new members for five years.

'Greaser says you've got enough fuel for a couple of hours at the very outside.'

'Plenty. If all goes to plan fifteen minutes should be enough.'

'That little?'

McNally shrugged. 'It's reassuring to have some in reserve in case we have to put her down somewhere else. I very much hope that won't happen.'

'What are the chances of that?'

Dhobi's glass stopped just short of his lips and his eyes searched McNally's face. A sudden wave of affection came over McNally. Funny old geezer. He'd miss the old buffer just as he would miss Hollywood and Lawless and Alice. Don't think too much about Alice. Not now.

'High.'

Both knew that if the Junkers landed anywhere other than its own field, arrest for the crew members would be certain.

'I mean. She's already landed at the wrong bloody airfield once, thanks to you and that lunatic Joystick Morgan.' McNally laughed but there was a manic edge to it.

'Let's hope for the best and prepare for the worst. I can't imagine Tschirner wanting a repeat performance of 1941 again.'

He caught Dhobi's look of surprise.

'Ah, come on now, Dhobi. Did you think I knew nothing about it? It's the leprechauns tell me these things. They can read thoughts and visit memories. There's one describing the picture to me right now. I can see a darkened runway and hear the throwing of a big switch which brings on the lights and in the distance the drone of an engine . . . no, two engines, one of them on the blink.

'I can see that old bugger hanging there on the wall as he was in life. Jesus, I bet he was insufferable, always throwing his weight around. Now the plane is getting nearer. The old fool thinks he's done his good deed for the day, but the young officer with him gives a cry as he identifies it as an enemy plane. By this time its wheels are down. At first Joystick is beside himself for having captured an enemy plane but the young duty officer has gone white as a sheet. "We've turned on the runway lights and attracted an enemy bomber," he says. "They'll shoot us for bloody treason!" This strikes an uncomfortable note with Joystick who anxiously asks "What's for the best?" A distinct note of rising concern in his voice. In a creditable display of lateral thinking before it was even called lateral thinking, the young officer – you – decides that the best thing is to pretend nothing has happened. It's a master stroke. All traces or records of the Junkers' arrival are obliterated and an elaborate cover story concocted about experimental flights and top-secret testings of a captured plane. The Junkers is then pushed into the back of the hangar and forgotten about. The crew are told to shove off and make their bewildered way into the village where the locals, thinking they are Poles or Dutch or Czech allies, grow to accept them.

'There are rumours, of course. After a while somebody darkly hints that Tschirner, Lang and Mutti could be English government spies sent to keep a watch-out for Welsh nationalism. Another old boy ups the scandal stakes even more. "I think they are German," he says. "What is the difference as far as we are concerned?" asks a third. "Between one kind of Hun and another? Let sleeping dogs lie, I say," and the subject is dropped not to be resurrected for over half a century. That's pretty much what happened, wasn't it? The most argumentative and possibly the luckiest

Luftwaffe aircrew ever to have been downed over Britain have lived to fight another day. And today is that day.'

The magic lamp of Dhobi's memory lit up and now the old man smiled at the ancient memories which had been released.

'The ghost crew,' he said slowly. 'The lot of you. Undocumented and without real existence. And an old plane flying out of a time warp. Ghosts. Bloody ghosts.'

They drank slowly and quietly for a while, McNally thinking that one day he would get the story in its every detail. It was an amazing story. He shook his head wondering if there was anything else Dhobi had concealed. Surely there had been women in Tschirner's and Lang's lives? And Mutti? One long night he'd pump Dhobi for the full, unexpurgated version. He promised himself that for the future. Always assuming there was to be a future.

'You're going to miss Alice.'

Dhobi had saved the statement, which was really a question, until last. A couple of times now McNally had noticed Dhobi sounding a bit like a concerned uncle every time Alice came into the conversation.

'I should have known you'd know. It's over between Alice and me. Regardless of what happens to me she'll stay in Maescwm with Lawless. She's fascinated by me, for some reason. But she loves Lawless. Anyway, they enjoy having their teeth locked in one another's necks. They deserve each other.' The cheeriness in his voice rang false.

'I don't want to sound old fashioned but it's the gentlemanly thing to do. Lawless likes you, you know, in his way.'

McNally smiled. 'I'd hate to see what he does to people he can't stand.'

Dhobi excused himself to make some phone calls. McNally read for a bit and then sat in the sun with a soft drink but found that no matter how much he tried to distract himself he was drawn back to the Junkers.

He was sat in the old canvas chair after his umpteenth visit to the hangar when Alice tapped him on the shoulder.

'A penny for them?'

'They're not worth that much. Just thinking about the flight. How it'll go. What will happen afterwards. The rest of my life. Little things like that.' He tried a devil-may-care smile but it came out all twisted.

'Go on. Tell me.'

Suddenly McNally found himself saying all the things he'd silently sworn not to say. Worse, as anxiety tripped over anxiety, the words came gushing out.

'I'm worried sick about you having the worst job of the lot. You'll have to get him out of the bunker by half-past eight to be on the safe side. Will you promise me something, Alice? Get out of there yourself even if he stays behind. I can just about live with his blood on my hands. But you . . . if anything happened . . .'

He felt a hot tear forming in the corner of his eye.

She took his hand for an instant. 'You're frightened for me as well as for yourself and I'm touched, but you do your job and I'll do mine.'

He took her hand and kissed it gently. 'You're really in the front line. As much as me and Tschirner and Lang.'

'I wouldn't be there if I hadn't volunteered. Don't go soft on me, McNally. Anyway. You won't think so much of me when I say what I have to.'

She sat on the grass beside him with her back against the peeling drab-olive hangar wall.

'I'm going to patch things up with Lawless. I'm sorry if that hurts you but we're all getting a little too old for this kind of excitement. I kind of feel that after tonight some things will change for good even if the flying club is saved.

147

It's a night for making decisions and that's mine. I'm besotted with you, McNally, but that's my tough luck. The sex part's over.'

'So Snilesworth will be the last one to have a crack at you before domesticity settles in?'

'Don't be like a spoilt baby.' Alice spoke through pouted lips. 'That's different. It's for the cause. I expect that if we do get that far I won't enjoy it.'

'I've no right to be jealous. I shouldn't care. Just make sure that when you hear the sound of that aeroplane you're out of the bunker and in the main building. How you manage that is up to you.'

'Better illicitly in bed than dead?'

'Something like that.'

Alice stood up, handed McNally back the soft drink can and brushed stray bits of grass from her skirt. As he viewed her progress towards the clubhouse a confusing series of thoughts ran riot through McNally's mind like a pack of Wolf Cubs in a sweet factory. The Junkers, high on its sturdy undercarriage which had given it the capacity to land on the roughest frontline airfields was a part of it and so was she. He tried to imagine the force of the blast and then began to worry about the secondary damage that might be caused to the house in which Snilesworth and Alice would be ensconced.

Hollywood jumped into the picture and out again. He thought of his life in Maescwm, the Grapes of Wrath and Megan and whether they would keep his old car for him. He would ask somebody to park it in the hangar safe against the day of his return. All these things were part of it but there was something else at the back of it all, niggling him like a stone in his shoe.

It was Greaser. Alice and the Junkers aircrew were players in the drama which was about to unfold but Greaser was the villain waiting in the wings. The mechanic must know everything. What he hadn't been told he would be able to guess. McNally tried to judge how much was Greaser's thirty pieces of silver.

To escape this thought he was glad to enter the hangar and look at the bomber.

Everybody had gone. There was just him and it.

She was beautiful, no doubt about it. And deadly. He took in the two large engine nacelles, each containing mighty Jumos, actually in-line engines despite the round radiators which made them look like radials, a fact betrayed by the row of stubby exhaust pipes on the outer nacelle.

On the underside she had been painted a surprisingly bright blue. Not like the Germans to get the correct shade of the average British summer sky wrong. Dull slate grey would have been better. On the top side she wore a mottled drab pattern. On her fuselage the black cross stood out stark. The hard symmetry of the swastika covered half the tailplane. She was fuelled and bombed-up and ready to go, a thing of the air soon to take to its element.

Even before the voice he knew someone was there.

'McNally?' It was Alice's voice disembodied by the darkness of the hangar, sending out small echoes in the cavernous space.

'I'm scared. For you, and for me and for Tschirner.'

'Tschirner? He's the happiest of all.' McNally answered back to the darkness. 'I think he'd fly straight into the bunker if it weren't for the chance that you might still be inside.'

'I like to think he would consider me. He's my father.'

McNally spun round, seeking Alice's face which would prove he hadn't imagined it, but there was only the echoing slam of the hangar's side door.

Chapter Seventeen

No marching bands, no parades, no flags or bugles had marked the closure of RAF station, Maescwm.

It was a little bit of flotsam beached after the high tide of war had passed, too insignificant for the government to stoop and pick up. On its last day as an RAF station, the orderly sergeant had hauled down the ensign and tossed it to an aircraftsman in the back of a truck. The last official RAF presence driving out the main gate had passed the band of foraging villagers in carts and lorries and vans, equipped with cutting torches, screwdrivers and any other implement useful in the task of relieving the unwanted base of its fixtures and fittings. Officially, the land reverted to the county council upon which 'Joystick' Morgan had been serving as chairman of the all-important planning committee since 1935.

Several post-war property speculators had applied to buy the old airfield from the council for housing but inexplicably had been blocked by the planning committee without possibility of appeal.

The problem of what to do with the Junkers had given Flying Officer Thomas a chance to exercise the administrative skills which would later make his name a byword for laundry and billeting officers throughout the RAF. The task of concealing a twin-engined long range bomber was one to test even such a thoroughgoing bender of rules and cooking of books as the man later to be known as 'Dhobi' Thomas, the nickname taken from the Indian word for laundry and incorporated into services slang.

His solution had been a bureaucratic tour de force touched by genius. In the middle of the night young Flying Officer Thomas sat bolt upright in bed and shouted out the number of an RAF form, thus severely startling the commanding officer's wife adulterously snuggled beside him.

'I'll put it in amongst the rabbits. I'll hide it amongst the bloody rabbits!' he had shouted ecstatically as the alarmed woman hastily scrambled into her frock and bolted for the bedroom door.

The plan was as simple as it was ingenious.

With military logic the RAF classified everything it owned, from four-motor Lancaster bombers right down to hairpins for aircraftwomen, using a system that put the generic name of the thing to be classified first.

Thus a 'Pin, Hair, WAAF' appeared after 'Pin, Grenade, Explosive' but before 'Pin, Rolling'.

By precisely the same logic, 'Hurricane, Fighter Aircraft' appeared in official paperwork next to 'Hurricane, Lamp'.

It was a wonderful system that mixed things up costing hundreds of thousands, if not millions of pounds with things worth a few coppers. And as Thomas pulled on his Trousers, Battledress, Officers' and snapped his Braces, Men's into place and slid the customary two quid for the use of the room under the receptionist's bell he reflected that it was one perfectly designed for his nefarious purpose.

By the time he was in his illegally requisitioned Truck, General Purpose, Quarter-Ton and heading back to Maescwm he was whistling, for the plan was beginning to consolidate nicely.

The very next morning after he had mystified the commanding officer with an especially crisp salute and peculiar smile he had made for the office where the station's inventory was kept and opened it at the letter P.

It was several columns before he got to 'Plane', but his heart skipped with excitement to find them at the bottom of a page. The list started at 'Plane, Jack, Carpentry' leaving room for one more line to be typed before it turned over to 'Plane, Rabbeting'.

With fumbling fingers he released the page and carried it like an ancient and invaluable parchment to the corporal typist and instructed him to type in a new line after jack planes but before rabbeting planes.

The corporal, wise in the ways of officers and anyway due to be demobbed in ten days' time, shrugged and put the inventory sheet into his wide carriage typewriter and tapped away.

Within minutes 'Plane, Junkers, German' had been inserted in its correct alphabetical position and the page replaced.

Thomas then withdrew another file which listed all items which were to be disposed of locally and not returned to RAF central stores, and added all planes to the list. With a massive demobilization of men and materials under way, and even lorries falling off the back of lorries, nobody was going to bother about a few woodworking tools.

He then typed out an order putting the smaller of the two hangars in which the Junkers was hidden out of bounds and arranged for signs warning of mines to be placed all around it.

He had placed this before the commanding officer who had signed it without looking at the order and his arrangements were complete.

The seat upon which McNally was slumped was one of the few movable items left by pillaging villagers after the RAF had gone.

It was a tubular steel and canvas affair removed from a prehistoric Avro Anson aircraft many years before by ground crew and installed in their rest room as a novelty item of furniture.

The rest room – crew room in RAF parlance – was tucked just inside the hangar's huge doors and apart from the seat, contained a couple of rickety chairs left over from the briefing, a portable gas stove and kettle, some semi-pornographic pin-ups and a collection of actually porno-graphic ones to which witty captions had been appended or artistic alterations made. One nubile young woman being serviced in an unorthodox manner that had nothing whatsoever to do with the servicing of aircraft, had Holly-wood's head attached.

The picture had led to a minor artistic skirmish between Hollywood and Lawless.

Shrewdly guessing that the artist was to blame, Holly-wood had obtained a photograph of Lawless with his mouth wide open about to demolish a pint of beer and had replaced the pint he was grasping with a portion of anatomy that is exclusively male.

Thus, to the general amusement of all, had honour on both sides been satisfied.

A pile of spent matches was scattered by the gas burner where McNally had been making himself coffees and smok-ing, activities designed to keep his mind on the job.

Just as he mentally had the Junkers lined up for the kill, thoughts of Alice would jump him and engage his thoughts in dogfights.

Over and over again the words 'He's my father' emerged from the turmoil of the battle.

Tschirner, his pilot, was her father. He could see how it might be. The young stranger coming to Maescwm with very little English but with the quick-wittedness of the combat flier. Of course he would be attractive to women

153

and in a little place like Maescwm his very foreignness would make him more so. Who was the mother? he wondered. Alice had never spoken of uncles, aunts, nephews and cousins normal in the extended Welsh family. Perhaps she'd been an officer's wife spending the war in the relative safety of Wales and had fallen for Tschirner's charms, or at least fallen victim to his needs.

Why had she not mentioned it before? He tried to think back about how Alice and Tschirner were together but could not recall any special warmth. If anything, Tschirner had always been rather reserved in her presence, which he had put down to German correctness. This line of thought fizzled out in too many possibilities. Time enough for sorting out the tangled roots of the Tschirner/Alice family tree after the attack.

His mind switched back to the Junkers where he was in the bomb-aimer's position, watching the ground speeding by beneath him, the slight rock of turbulence and his shouted commands to the pilot. He breathed deeply and cleared his mind of all except what the next few hours would bring. The crew room was warm, its walls releasing the pungent whiff of thousands of pairs of oily dungarees and Woodbines absorbed during the years of RAF occupation. Too many things racing through his mind were tiring him and his brain began to send strong signals to his body that it should take a nap.

'Don't worry about bombshells in your personal life,' was its final message. 'When you will soon be dealing with bombshells of a much more tangible kind.'

McNally had been gazing at the porno picture amusingly doctored by Lawless before he nodded off.

It was the live version of the same face now leaning over him and shaking him awake.

'It's time. The others are waiting for you,' said Hollywood.

This was what the condemned man really felt like, the thought flashed through his mind, as it had several times before but never with the same terrifying sense of reality. His mouth tasted metallic and when he stood there was a weakness in his knees. At any moment the chaplain intoning prayers would enter the crew room accompanied by the prison governor in his best hanging suit.

The Junkers was being wheeled out into the fast-fading light.

A small knot of club members stood about twenty yards away from the aircraft. Lang and Tschirner were by its wing.

A hundred yards of tarmac lay between McNally and the plane. He began the walk still feeling dizzy, ashamed of the tremble in his knee. In Maescwm village the first of the lights were coming on. High clouds were still tinged with pink and there was little wind.

Lang greeted him with an affable smile and ground out a cigarette.

'*Heil Hitler!*' Tschirner said with a smile which was an almost imperceptible pressing of his lips as he made a joke of the old Nazi greeting.

Or at least McNally supposed it was a joke and nodded back.

The door on the underside of the Junkers was open with the aluminium ladder leading up into the aircraft's belly. McNally entered first, feeling life in the airframe around him.

Lang followed but Tschirner delayed an instant.

McNally knew that he was scanning the faces of the watchers, looking for Alice but she was already at Snilesworth's place. As he entered the Junkers the dim electric light made the old man look very sad.

Through the plexiglass nose, McNally could see the watchers waving. He too wished Alice was there but he knew that even now she was with Snilesworth, probably in his arms, kissing him with a Judas kiss.

The Junkers rocked slightly as Tschirner climbed aboard. A small pressure wave hit McNally's eardrums as the blister was shut and locked. The sound was halfway between a crack and a thrash as first the starboard engine caught, followed by its partner. He listened to the beat of the engines and fancied that the port, the one that had been damaged, was running rougher than its brother, but dismissed it as nerves.

The pilot and co-pilot were shouting above the noise of the engines, an old but remembered routine. Tschirner released the brakes and with deft touches of rudder and throttle brought the Junkers to the beginning of the runway, straining against the brakes.

The roar of the engines reached a crescendo and the ancient airframe began to vibrate so that McNally feared the rivets would pop. He watched the grass being flattened by the propwash, waving and thrashing like some strange, alien sea.

The clothes of the wavers were blown to the contours of their bodies. McNally picked out Mutti, who was waving a handkerchief and who appeared to be weeping and also Hollywood. He could not see Greaser.

Tschirner released brakes and the old aeroplane surged forward. Here and there tussocks of grass had forced their way through cracks in the runway's surface but as the Junkers built up speed the bumps became fewer and less pronounced and suddenly they were airborne.

McNally looked down from his position in the nose as Tschirner made a wide turn and came back over Maescwm airfield and those below waving and cheering.

The last thing McNally saw as Tschirner set his course was BOLLOX's wall. The last message had been scrubbed and a new one substituted.

GOOD BUY AND GOOD RIDDENCE

The prospect of battle was making the blood run hot in his veins. How he would love to ... how he would just bloody love to ... a little more to the right and a little lower and he would be able to lob a bomb right into the nest of BOLLOX cretins. To hell with them. Get this business with Snilesworth over and let them wither on the vine.

Tschirner banked the aircraft slightly and powered it towards the bunker, a vast black-crossed avenging angel.

Chapter Eighteen

'IT'S A GERMAN PLANE FLYING AT TREE-TOP HEIGHT AND GOING LIKE SHIT OFF A HOT SHOVEL . . . DO YOU READ ME?'

Police Constable Meurig Pritchard's lack of official radio protocol was due to the fact that his BMW patrol bike was up-ended in a muddy ditch with him pinned under it.

The plane had passed so close that he had smelled the heat of its exhausts. 'OF COURSE I WANT ASSISTANCE. I'M TRAPPED UNDER MY BIKE IN A STINKING DITCH WITH A BROKEN BLOODY ARM . . .'

He let go of the transmit button and sank back into the ooze for a few seconds, exhausted. The radio crackled into life and with superhuman effort he brought the microphone to his face once more.

'UH? WHAT? A HEINKEL OR A DORNIER OR SOMETHING. ONE OF THOSE YOU SEE IN THE WAR FILMS. HOW DO I KNOW IT WASN'T AN RAF JET? TWO THINGS. ONE IT WASN'T A JET AND TWO IT HAD SWASTIKAS ALL OVER IT YOU FUCKING MORON.' PC Pritchard dropped the mike again and began to sob with pain and frustration.

As police parlance had it, he had been proceeding in a southerly direction on the B4358 three miles to the west of the village of Maescwm when a World War Two German aeroplane came hell for leather from somewhere behind him and frightened him off his bike.

It had roared away in the direction of Mynydd Maen. Since he and the bike were spinning through the air at the time he couldn't be sure of it, but he had sensed, rather than actually saw, an explosion some miles away. What, he wondered, was Control finding so difficult to comprehend about that?

Now the silly bastards were asking for a map reference, as though he had worked out a spot on the ordnance survey map and decided to crash right there.

Feebly, he told the control room that he was temporarily unable to locate a map, compass or satellite beacon. That being the case, why didn't they get off their arses and send somebody to look for his skidmarks by the side of the road? Several cars, any of which might have stopped and helped, had passed but Pritchard and the wrecked bike were invisible below the edge of the ditch.

It was getting dark and a dangerous chill was beginning to invade his body.

Early attempts to lift the weight of the bike from his arm had only resulted in his being forced further down to the slime but now he managed to get his back against the relatively firm bank and with an excruciating effort to push the machine away.

The ditch was steep, with only a few straggly weeds to afford a handhold. Several times he grabbed hold of one of the stouter growths only to have it come away in his hand. Once he managed to get his good arm over the top of the bank but the toehold he had kicked in the soft earth gave way, sending him slithering back into the ooze.

In the slide down, Pritchard's helmet had scooped up a dense packing of mud which threatened his hearing and, more importantly, his breathing.

He fingered it away and listened to the sound of police sirens in the distance.

In the gathering dark he fancied he could see blue flashing lights. With one titanic effort which induced a scream of pain he clawed himself to the top of the bank, feet kicking wildly and one arm flailing, a last desperate fight which consumed every last ounce of strength.

In a storm of light and sound the police cars screamed past scattering a shower of grit in his face. When they had passed, their lights now a mere flicker in the distance, PC Meurig Pritchard lowered his head into the crook of his arm and for the first time in thirty-eight years began to cry for his mother.

From his position looking downwards through the plexiglass nose of the Junkers, McNally saw the flashing lights of the police cars and knew they had been betrayed.

Now was not the time to think about that. The darkening fields were flashing beneath the belly of the aeroplane. In less than a minute they would be over the target.

He had spotted the pale rectangular light emitting from the bunker half a minute before and so had Tschirner, who had put the Junkers on a perfect line for the bombing run.

At that speed and from that height the bomb would not drop through the skylight but smash into the wall with a slingshot effect. Before they had taken off they had received the signal that Alice and Snilesworth had left the bunker.

He prayed that it was so and snuggled his eye against the bombsight. The excitement was orgiastic. Blood pounded in his temples and his every nerve tuned to what he could see. McNally knew that nothing would stop him dropping the bomb.

'Steady . . . left . . . steady . . . steadyyyyyyyyy . . . YES!'

An instant after he pressed the toggle, the aircraft skipped and he knew the bomb had dropped clear.

'I want to see inside the main house,' she had said petulantly and stuck out her lower lip.

Snilesworth knew a good bargaining hand when he saw one and had relented immediately.

They were in the house by eight thirty and in bed by eight forty-five. By eight fifty-seven when her ears picked up the sound of an approaching aircraft, he was grunting a rapid progress towards orgasm.

His orgasm started as a tingling, a feeling that all the sensations his body had ever experienced were coming together in one spot.

Alice knew that her job was to keep him in the bedroom for as long as possible to allow for any delay in take off, which meant faking it. Snilesworth had installed a television monitor high on the wall which is how she knew the time to be eight fifty-nine and thirty seconds. The idiot, dead eye of the remote control camera was flicking around the bunker's great emptiness. The drone of the plane was becoming a roar and she could tell from its throatiness that it was the Junkers.

Snilesworth was gritting his teeth and arching his back, only the tip of his manhood inside her. He wore a look of strained concentration like a baby dumping in its nappy. It was going to be a thirty-seconds job. Alice's thoughts were inside the Junkers and seeing her father, Lang and McNally, their faces also taut with concentration.

Any second now. Please, McNally, aim well . . .

'OH, OH, THAT'S IT. COME ON. I'M COMING OH . . . YES. THAT'S IT. OH, PERFECT!' The roar of the aircraft reached an ear-splitting crescendo. Snilesworth, oblivious in his lust, was thrashing in ecstasy and whimpering. Nothing now could conquer that tickle, that primeval

161

uncoiling somewhere within him that had now spread and taken over every nerve in his body.

A tenth of a second later it was as though the side of the house had been hit by a dozen bulldozers all going at one hundred miles an hour.

As if in slow motion a huge crack traced itself across the ceiling. Plaster dust and small bits of rubble mixed with the sweat on Snilesworth's back so that he resembled an animated, shagging statue.

'YEEEEESS! YES! YES! YES! OH, YES! DID THE EARTH MOVE FOR YOU?' he screamed.

'No.'

Now it was over Alice was completely detached.

'But the ceiling just did.'

Chapter Nineteen

A dirty orange flash bloomed at the centre of the blast. McNally looked below and behind to see the walls of the bunker bulge and split like a ripe Camembert cheese smacked with the flat of a cricket bat.

The Junkers jinked as the shock wave caught it and rode it along with a howl of triumph from McNally, scorer of the perfect, one-time shot. He looked to see if Tschirner was laughing but the pilot was scanning the instruments in front of him and looking preoccupied.

Not that even in this ecstatic moment McNally particularly wanted to meet Tschirner's eyes. He felt a mixture of shame and bewilderment in the presence of the father of the woman he had been sleeping with, on and off, for the past three years, and who had just come within a whisker of being blasted off the face of the planet.

That was assuming she had got out of the bunker. What if the lookout for the main house had been mistaken? Panic momentarily struck before being driven away by a real and more pressing anxiety.

The port engine was packing up.

It looked and sounded sick, trailing oily smoke and firing only intermittently.

Lang was also looking out at it and Tschirner, who had the controls, was looking forward, his eyes quartering the darkening sky ahead as they fought to make altitude.

'Will we make it?' McNally could not make out Lang's actual words but got the drift.

Tschirner replied in the affirmative. The failing engine had still been able to contribute in giving the aircraft height and now Tschirner was trimming her to fly as easily as possible.

With a slight shock McNally realized that Tschirner and Lang had been speaking German.

'The aircraft can easily fly on one engine and we are not now loaded.' Tschirner now spoke in English.

He was not sure whether the remark was addressed to him or Lang. Anyway, it was reassuring to know.

Coolly, Tschirner made a wide sweeping turn to the right. McNally tried hard not to think about the instruments in front of the pilots which would show oil pressure in the port engine dropping away almost to nothing and an alarmingly diminishing fuel supply.

'I think we are in for a different welcome from the sort we had envisaged. Look down there.'

McNally and Lang followed Tschirner's glance down towards Maescwm Flying Club.

The clubhouse was held in the beam of car headlamps and blue flashing lights were everywhere.

Shit. This was the work of that treacherous bastard, Greaser.

From what they could see, club members who would have welcomed them back and ushered them to safety had been replaced by squads of policemen standing by cars, vans and motorcycles. A light but fast aircraft with the word POLICE on the fuselage sides and on top of the high wing was taxiing on to the main runway.

This was it. Game up. McNally pictured himself standing in the dock at the Crown Court in Cardiff listening to the charges. Aerial arson. Waging war against Her Majesty's peace. Industrial sabotage. Conspiring with others to fly an aircraft in a dangerous manner. Displaying swastikas, black crosses and such other devices as to cause alarm to Her Majesty's subjects. Carrying an offensive weapon, to whit, a 500-kilogram bomb. Unauthorized use of explosives. Unauthorized alterations to a building contrary to the local authority building regulations. Taking and flying an aircraft without notifying air traffic control. Being Irish, with moderate Republican sympathies. And, the little irrelevancy sprang to mind, the excise licence on his car had just run out.

Strangely, the sight of the blue uniforms seemed to amuse Tschirner, who so far had flown with complete professional detachment.

'Ah. The Tommies are waiting for us, do you see that, Lang?' he said with what, in ex-Nazis, passed for a smile.

'*Ja.* I see. But I think this time we shall not be so cooperative?'

The old men looked at one another, excluding McNally from their conversation. They were back more than fifty years in time. The police aeroplane had reached the end of the runway and was now beginning to roll. In a minute it would be airborne and shadowing them. Blue smoke was streaming from the sick engine as Tschirner turned the Junkers in a wide circle. Miraculously, he was still able to coax some power from it.

It was only after the turn had been completed that Tschirner's intention dawned upon McNally.

The Junkers was now roaring towards the runway towards the Piper, full throttle and at no more than fifteen feet. Through the plexiglass he could see the Piper gaining speed.

They were going to ram it! The mad German bastards were going to go down in a ball of fire, a *Götterdämmerung*, one terrible, flaming moment of smashed and burning metal, a fireball of aviation gasoline, five men simultaneously and spectacularly transported to the feasting halls of Valhalla! Insanely he found himself glancing at his watch. Four minutes past nine. Only four minutes after the bombing run. Probably a good time to join Thor at his feasting-board. Just as the lads slain in battle were coming down to breakfast after a hard night's pillaging and raping.

In one instant, which for all intents and purposes Mc-Nally took to be his last, he saw the white face of the police pilot. In the absence of any Teutonic prayers the words of the Hail Mary burbled from his lips. Then his soul sailed heavenwards to meet his Maker. So this was what it was like. Sort of a hangover from life. He was in the Junkers but . . . dead. McNally was surprised that corpses felt the pull of G-forces and that things around him persisted in being so solid.

The roaring climb of the Junkers was real enough and so were the exultant shouts of Lang and Tschirner. The engine was still smoking away materially. He was dying for a cigarette. Weren't you supposed to leave vices like that at the Pearly Gates? He felt sure Heaven would be a no-smoking area. On the other hand, if they were on their way to Valhalla with the Junkers as their own personal Valkyrie, sin was probably mandatory.

'Did you see that! We forced the Piper back down on the runway! It will be minutes before he is after us and we will have gone – phut!' Tschirner bawled over the engine noise.

McNally, who for several moments had thought they had already gone 'phut', ferreted in the left pocket of his A–2 and pulled out his Embassy Number Ones and the old Zippo and lit the cigarette with trembling hand. Bugger flight safety.

Tschirner had feathered the port propeller and put the Junkers back in level flight. Now the excitement had passed to be replaced by calm. Odd, McNally reflected, that a man flying on one engine in a Junkers bomber having just dropped a 500-kilogram bomb on a peaceful country and who by now had every policeman in Wales after him should be feeling this way, but he did.

He eased himself into a space behind the pilot's and co-pilot's seats and read the compass-bearing as a few degrees west of north. The Black Mountains were a fading line, undistinguishable from the low cloud tinged by evening behind them. Lights shone from cottages on the eastern slopes of hills and in the deepest valleys where night had already fallen. Here and there tractors and cars crept across the land like little glow-worms. White-painted farmhouses glowed pink in the fading light and once they flew over a tiny castle on a steep hilltop, the white flecks of sheep clustered by its walls looking no bigger than ants' eggs.

A jolt of anxiety hit McNally and brought his heart right up to speed. No way could that calm last. There had only been half an hour's fuel left, according to Greaser. He scanned the instrument board for the fuel gauge and saw that it was on empty.

Lang saw his anxiety and turned in his seat and smiled.

The smile was very, very worrying. It was eloquent body language which said, 'We've come to the end of the road and do you know what? I don't give a damn.'

Tschirner's face remained ahead to where mountains loomed blue and ancient.

'Where are we going to put her down?' McNally's mind had run through the possibilities and had come up with one probability.

The possibilities were the airport at Merseyside, the RAF station at Valley and a couple of small fields used by gliding clubs. Since the Junkers did not have radios to obtain the necessary clearance for landing, such options seemed unattractive at best and outright suicidal at worst. Crash-landing was also an option, but one equally fraught. Tschirner and Lang were probably crazed but they were not homicidal

167

maniacs so far as he could judge. The valley floor was spotted with little farms and cottages. Ploughing into one of them and whisking the occupants away to a premature salvation was therefore a real prospect. For simple hill folk accustomed to asking the Lord for their daily bread, several tons of World War Two Junkers suddenly bursting through the front door seemed a bit harsh.

Those were the possibilities.

Something about Tschirner's expression made him think that the likelihood was something much more dramatic and terminal. He was sure that in one last terrible gesture Tschirner was going to plunge the old aircraft and them into the mountainside. He wondered if now was the time to bring up the matter of Alice's parentage. Probably not. On the other hand, there were a couple of minutes of life left to them.

'About Alice. I'm sorry. For everything. I didn't know she was your daughter.'

He was bawling into Tschirner's ear and was surprised when the old man turned and smiled.

'It does not matter so much. We are men and women and we cannot avoid what the fates have in store for us. It was fate that you should meet my daughter and that such a thing should happen between you. She is very much like her mother to whom I was greatly attracted.'

'Evidently.'

'What? Anyway. The time has come to confront our destiny. We shall all meet it together, yourself, myself and Lawless's father.'

'Say again?' McNally's shout was tight and shrill with amazement. He cupped his ear, sure that the stuttering of the starboard engine had made him hear incorrectly.

'Oh yes. Lang is Lawless's father. You did not know this?'

'I don't believe it!' McNally dumped himself on the vibrating metal floor to recover. The Junkers was a flying gene-pool headed for oblivion. This was the moment when your life was supposed to flash before your eyes.

All right. Flash, you bugger.

Nothing much came up. A few faces of people he'd known only briefly, which was puzzling. Perhaps they were the people sent by Fate to have an impact on his life but who somehow hadn't made it.

Funny thing, Fate. If you couldn't recognize the signals it was sending you what was the point of its being? Oh well. The question was a trifle philosophical now.

In a few minutes at the most the whole secret of life and death would be gloriously revealed.

'I'm sorry. Both of you. I . . . didn't know.'

The last of the roseate light was touching a large sheet of water which must be Lake Bala. There was still light enough to see people by the lakeside, looking up at the plane's fiery progress.

'There isn't time to explain.'

'True enough, McNally. Lang and I are doing now what would have happened all those years ago if Joystick Morgan and Dhobi had not turned on the runway lights and given us a new lease on life. Now that lease has run out. It has been a good life, has it not, Lang?'

'*Ja.* Sure. Coming to Maescwm was like coming home. And of course there are the children to be grateful for. So talented.'

'Why didn't you tell me about Alice and Lawless?'

Neither Tschirner nor Lang looked away from the lake, so near now that McNally could see the ripples.

Lang shrugged.

'In wartime in an enemy country you lay low and say little, even in Maescwm where talking is a way of life. After the war I suppose we got out of the habit of saying much about our affairs.'

Now Tschirner spoke.

'You will have noticed that the bomb doors are open. Your relative youth has purchased you a choice. If you jump while we are low over the water you will have a good chance of survival.'

Idiotically, McNally's mind was more concerned with Tschirner's pronunciation of 'survival' which came out like 'surwival'.

'About your daughter. And Lawless . . .'

'Ah, yes. There is a condition to this. I think Alice should be spared your further attentions. Lang and I would both like that. Is it a deal?'

'I'm not just saying this. Alice and I had agreed it anyway. She loves Lawless.'

'Good. *Auf wiedersehn*, then, McNally.'

He clambered to the rear and looked down through the bomb bay at the speeding water.

One touch of his Zippo for luck and McNally dropped into the maelstrom of thrashing air and atomized oil, the water coming at him as hard-looking as sheet steel.

Chapter Twenty

Instinct told him to curl up into a ball to meet the water which any second now was going to deliver a heavyweight knockout punch.

The impact caught his shoulders with a mighty blow, uncurling him and slamming the breath from his body. McNally burst coughing and spluttering to the surface just in time to see the last seconds of the Junkers. Tschirner had glided the length of the lake unconcerned to even try and ditch the plane. McNally dog-paddled, fascinated.

At that speed they would die even if they did try and bring her down in the lake. A picture of the old aeroplane being hauled from the lake's depths with pallid corpses still in the pilot and co-pilot seats invaded his mind's eye for a split second.

The lake, with its Celtic gods would not be the place for those two. Tschirner and Lang were going to commend themselves to the sterner gods of their Teutonic ancestors. The thought of the two argumentative old warriors being transported back to their flaxen-haired youth obliged to work their way through a fresh crop of virgins every day tickled him somehow. This train of thought, strangely beyond grieving or even awe at the spectacle unfolding in front of him, continued as the Junkers' left wingtip caught a bluff, sending the machine spinning like a giant Catherine wheel. The sound reached him two seconds after the bloom of fire which struck the hillside like a lightning bolt hurled by a wrathful god. For fully half a minute afterwards incandescent pieces of debris cascaded down into the lake and fired bracken at the foot of the bluff.

People had gathered on the shore as he began the swim. The water was killingly cold and the full, blouse shape of his leather jacket dragged but the distance was not great and he decided against abandoning it. Neither had he dumped his boots, a decision which had made for an exhausting swim but one which, as he pulled himself ashore on to a rough pebble beach, he was pleased he had made. Pausing to rest for only a minute he commenced the walk towards the dull glow at the bottom of the hill.

Two fire tenders and a police car hee-hawed past. Instinctively he ducked into the shadows every time a police or emergency vehicle rushed by. By the time he reached the scene the torches and searchlights and the blue flashing lights of the emergency vehicles were already eclipsing the dimming fires of the Junkers.

Already police were cordoning off the wreckage but the lights were making deep pools of shadow in which McNally could inch himself nearer to the charred and twisted remains.

Nothing remained of the forward part of the fuselage where Tschirner and Lang had been. The central part and wings inboard of the engines had gone but the tailplane and outer wings were recognizable. The swastika on the tailplane had been only partially obliterated. McNally guessed the engines had been rammed ten feet into the mountainside by their own weight.

Policemen in blue dungarees were combing the vicinity for wreckage and twice McNally had to slide into the cover of a gorse bush to escape discovery.

A drab olive-green Land Rover bumped and lurched up the track leading back in the direction of Bala, the yellow stripe running horizontally at headlight height, indicating that it belonged to the Royal Air Force. An officer wearing combat clothes and a peaked cap, and a driver similarly clad but with a beret slammed the car's doors and hurried towards a knot of senior police officers.

McNally crept to within earshot. He was surprised that the policemen were not discussing the black crosses displayed on what was left of the aircraft. Perhaps, quite simply, they could not believe the evidence of their eyes.

They seemed glad at first, when the RAF man joined them. 'It's definitely not one of ours,' were the RAF officer's first words. McNally guessed he had been sent down from the RAF station at Valley.

'The swastika and the black crosses on the wing had rather suggested that to us already,' the tallest and most senior of the police replied crisply. The other RAF person smiled behind the officer's back. McNally saw it was a girl.

'Well, you know. We do have curios.' But the tall policeman had turned away and was talking into a radio.

'A chap was sent round to the RAF museum at Hendon to make sure the Junkers 88 and the Dornier were . . . um . . . still there. We've spoken to the Civil Aviation Authority who say there is no Junkers 88 anywhere in Britain in private hands. It's a mystery, I'm afraid,' the RAF man continued despite the snub.

The superintendent clicked off his radio but spoke in the taut tone he had used before.

'We don't like mysteries. Too many people ask too many questions and generate too much paperwork. And that is a strain on our budget, Flight Lieutenant.'

Grey, glacial eyes that had surveyed the carnage of a thousand embittered meetings with Home Office and county council officials turned upon the RAF officer.

'Not that we are going to be particularly overburdened in this case. The police and, ah, other security agencies with whom we occasionally work see no reason why the small irregularity concerning the aircraft's markings should prolong enquiries. If you get my meaning.'

The RAF man now seemed flustered, his pride forcing him to make a response.

'Irregularity! I'd hardly call swastikas on a modern-day aeroplane a mere irregularity! Anyway, the bloody thing must have come from somewhere.'

'If . . . you . . . get . . . my . . . meaning.'

The words were paced out with the authority of a policeman's footsteps.

'I think, Flight Lieutenant, that when you make your report you will find your superiors taking very much the same view as myself.'

The senior aircraftwoman who was stood some way back smiled.

'How many crew would she have had?' one of the other policemen asked, his tone more conciliatory.

'Three, possibly two. Both or all atomized by the impact or else buried so deep you'll have to dig away half the mountain to find the bits.'

McNally edged even nearer, so close he could smell the airwoman's perfume.

'Not teaching my grandmother, etcetera, but if word of this gets out, every souvenir-hunter in Britain will be here by daybreak. What are the police going to do about that?' The officer was determined to hold his own.

'And then there's the press. You're going to have to concoct a credible story for them.'

The Superintendent snorted, looking at his colleagues and inviting them to share in his contempt.

'The local press eats out of our hands.'

'Congratulations.' A wry note of confidence had crept into the officer's voice. The policeman had said a silly thing. He'd been delivered a chance to reverse his earlier humiliation and wasn't going to let it pass. 'But we're not talking about expired tax discs and nicking shoplifters at the local Spar. This is a story for the boys on the national papers. A World War Two German aircraft inexplicably crashing in North Wales is big, big, but big news. The reporters are going to want to know where the plane came from and who was in it. And when you can't tell them, Superintendent, there will be accusations of a cover-up.'

The Superintendent was on his back foot and didn't like it. McNally could feel the weight of his resentful silence from several feet away.

'So this is what we do.' The RAF man was pushing his advantage to the hilt.

'We cover the crosses and swastikas and keep security so tight a mouse couldn't creep through. The cover story is that the plane was a Russian-owned light commercial aircraft and we stick to it. People expect anything Russian-built to fall apart and the British press isn't going to be interested in a couple of dead foreigners. We'll put a police spokesperson in front of the cameras. Involving the RAF will only up the ante. With any luck by the time the press get on to this our accident investigation chaps will have this lot out of here and there'll only be a scorched patch of heather for journalists to look at. I think that's it for now, don't you?' With the policemen glowering after him the RAF officer beckoned to the girl and together they strolled off.

Fire-fighting foam shrouded the remains of the Junkers. There was nothing more for McNally to see.

When the coast was clear he edged away. The hills immediately surrounding the lake were not high and at first looked unpromising cover but eventually he found a small hollow which would shield the light from his fire. He knew that old stems of gorse would provide kindling. After they had caught, larger bits of wood could be added.

Keeping a careful watch, he fanned the little pyramid into flame. When an appreciable amount of warmth was radiating from the fire he removed the sodden cigarettes from their pack and laid them on a stone to dry.

When the fire was as high as he dared make it he built a crude frame from fallen branches and hung up his clothes to dry.

He was alive and uninjured, and had clothing. His couple of hundred pounds was useful but would have to be spent frugally. A pen, a few loose coins, a good aviator's watch and the much-loved Zippo completed the inventory. That was it. All he had left with which to start a new life.

McNally, one-time flying instructor, adulterer, temporary bomb-aimer, airborne arsonist, refugee from authority and imitator of the Barnes Wallis Bouncing Bomb was defined by such meagre possessions.

His underpants and vest dried quickly and it was pleasant to slip them on but the cotton cooled rapidly leaving him colder than before. He was glad when, much later, his wool shirt, trousers and socks were also dry and he was able to make a bed from bracken and retire, arranging his still-damp jacket over his shoulders.

Soon he was asleep on the hillside where Tschirner and Lang slept forever.

He awoke at first light, shivering in the grey nadir of the daily cycle when the skin feels gritty, a sense of foreboding prevails and all optimism is gone from a chill world.

At least the cigarettes were dry. He flicked the Zippo's knurled wheel and greedily sucked in the cigarette smoke, the warmth and familiar hardness of the lighter a comfort.

The temptation to go into Bala immediately and buy food at a newsagent would have to be resisted. He would wait until tourists were about to avoid being noticed. He was wildly dishevelled and had no comb, but in the middle of the morning, provided he seemed dry enough, the locals might mistake him for a hippy or one of the hermetic and crazed writers who were known to live among these hills.

He would get the *Western Mail*, too, for a report of the bombing. There had been no time to think of what mayhem had been left in the Junkers' wake but now the thought loomed large.

What if Alice had not after all coaxed Snilesworth from the bunker as the bomb blew it apart? Each minute seemed like an hour as with sepulchral slowness the colours came into the dawn and the hands of his watch ticked round to seven thirty.

At that time he decided he could stand it no longer. Stiff with cold and with the hardness of his bed he set off down the hillside for Bala village. A man and woman were leaving the black-and-white timbered enormousness of the White Lion Hotel for the lakeside. Two old men chatted in the road outside the old turreted market-place, staking their claim to the morning. A second before pushing open the door of what announced itself as the Siop Bapur Newydd at the junction of the main street and Heol Tegid, and next to the Lake View Chinese takeaway, McNally glanced at his reflection in the window.

The shop smelled of sweets and newsprint with coffee wafting from a room at the back, making him salivate. The five pound note had dried and as he took a *Western Mail*, a fresh-filled roll and two bars of chocolate, the young woman the other side of the counter regarded him without suspicion. A lot of deranged people made Wales their home and a fair percentage of them entered the shop. To her, he was nothing more than the first loony of the day.

His hands shook with excitement and at first his eyes overshot the story of the explosion a hundred miles south. It had been relegated to page five for the North Wales edition of the daily paper but it told him what he wanted to know.

Snilesworth, who had been in his country house a few hundred yards from his business premises had been 'relaxing at home' when the blast occurred. Neither he nor anyone else had been injured.

Suddenly the day seemed brighter. There was no mention of the crashed aircraft. That would be picked up by the evening papers which may or may not make a connection between the aircraft and the explosion near Maescwm. He muttered a quick prayer. Alice was safe.

Having taken in the headline and the first couple of paragraphs his eyes moved down the column. A 'mystery' explosion had completely levelled the registered offices of Dreemidwell Homes, causing secondary damage to the adjoining house.

In a brief statement a 'stunned' Snilesworth was reported as saying that, 'Several major projects in Wales, including a retail park which would have benefited nearby Maescwm village, would now have to be suspended while damage to the company's Welsh interests were assessed.'

A lengthy company profile by Neil Jones, the paper's business reporter, followed. It was a pithy piece in which the writer scarcely concealed a dislike for his subject. In an extract taken from an earlier interview Snilesworth boasted of his lack of formal education.

'I don't need education but I do need information,' he had said, unfolding his sterile personal philosophy. 'And that I can get from computers.'

'Past tense, Sunshine. *Could* get from computers!' McNally said out loud, causing the girl who had served him to eye him nervously.

'The businessman with the best electronic and information systems, the biggest and best database, is the one that stays ahead. I have seen the future and it's cybernetic.

Without the information highway you might as well be selling tomatoes from a barrow,' Snilesworth had intoned.

Sell tomatoes from a barrow then, you bastard. McNally folded the paper and threw it in the litter bin.

Snilesworth would be back. If not Maescwm then some other nice, quiet corner of Britain, lulled into believing that it had escaped the worst manifestations of the twentieth century would be visited by his awfulness.

Not for the first time McNally caught himself wishing that the bomb had blown Snilesworth to hell. Even there he'd probably set up a franchise deal selling buckets of water. In McNally's mind there could be no question of Snilesworth getting anywhere near the Pearly Gates.

The bugger would have them off their hinges, the pearls dug out and the rest melted down for scrap.

McNally bit hungrily into the fresh roll, strength and optimism now rampant. Snilesworth had been laid low and Alice was safe. It was certain that someone would make a connection between the Maescwm explosion and the Junkers. Police and RAF files would be consulted as well as those of the Civil Aviation Authority and the secret services, but they would all draw a mystifying blank. Tschirner and Lang had effectively ceased to exist when their Junkers failed to return after a bombing raid on Cardiff over fifty years before. The Luftwaffe aircrew that was no more had, in fact, never been.

The authorities could search their files and run their computers for as long as they liked but they would be chasing phantoms. All that remained was for him to tell Alice and Lawless of their fathers' last glorious, ghostly and anarchic mission.

Chapter Twenty-one

Maescwm Flying Club's committee sat in a solemn con-
clave, awkward and subdued in the presence of mourning.

Alice spoke little. Lawless was getting steadily drunk.
Dhobi pointed out that any sort of memorial service for
Tschirner and Lang would be risky since the proceedings
might be overheard by strangers.

'Absolutely! Even church walls have ears.' One elderly
member who had already despatched several large whiskies
as his own contribution to the mourning process managed
to enunciate, modifying the wartime slogan which swam to
the surface of his brain through the fog of fifty years and
an ocean of Scotch.

'Errr ... Keep mum ... She's not so dumb. I mean, it's
possible that the rozzers might have bally spies in the
cogrenation ... cogrent ... pews ... when the vicar does
his bit.'

A murmur of assent followed.

'Well ve most do something!' Mutti was tearful and
looked towards Hollywood for support.

'Zose men vor the varry foondations of this cloob.'

'Naff old mare,' Hollywood said under his breath, raising
his eyes. It was a relief in some ways there wouldn't be a
burial. He could picture Mutti throwing himself on one of
the coffins.

Nice the way he slipped in a bit of the native accent for effect, though. Very Marlene Dietrich.

'Ze varry foondations—'

'Careful, love. We all know the old Hollywood saying that if a thing's worth doing it's worth overdoing, but this is Maescwm and you can go too far.'

BBC Wales had followed up the story of the bombing, linking it with the mysterious German aircraft reported by police motorcyclist Meurig Pritchard a few moments before the conflagration.

PC Meurig Pritchard's own story had been recounted by the midday news from his hospital bed. The item attempted to link the crash with the Maescwm explosion, but this had been flatly denied by an official police spokeswoman.

The crashed aircraft had been Russian-owned with two Russian aircrew on board. There would be a full enquiry but early examination of the wreckage indicated mechanical failure.

The Maescwm explosion would be investigated as a separate incident. When a television reporter raised the matter of PC Pritchard's claim to have seen an old Luftwaffe plane flying at tree-top height minutes before the explosion, the spokeswoman put on her sweetest, most sympathetic smile.

'Police Constable Pritchard was very near the scene of the incident and was blown from his motorcycle by the force of the blast and severely concussed.'

Switching to a frown she had continued, 'It is regrettable that PC Pritchard had been pestered into making a statement while still suffering the effects of his injuries.'

Flicking back to the smile she had concluded, 'The officer will be spending a few days with his family after which he will make a full and formal statement. I'm sure we all wish Meurig a speedy recovery. That's all. Thank you.'

Sweeping up her papers she had then turned on her heel.

Alice and Lawless instinctively knew the truth. Though silent, Lawless had been drinking with a punishing intensity, his head moving from side to side like that of a poorly controlled dummy. He was dangerously volatile. It was like being in a room with a crate of weeping gelignite. A word uttered by Mutti had obviously penetrated Lawless's fuzzy brain and was ricocheting around.

'Foundations. Foundations. That's it,' he slurred, his voice like an unstable gravel-tip on the move.

A gargantuan fist slammed itself down on to the table.

'If we can't have the vicar we'll have a service of our own. We'll collect some personal possessions and bury them in the clubhouse's foundations. Mark of respect.'

His eyes moved jerkily and at different speeds round the table. Nobody thought it wise to disagree. Some rummaging around the clubhouse and a visit to the dead fliers' homes had within the hour produced Lang's Luftwaffe eagle insignia, two bar bills, a black and white snapshot of the two Germans at a club picnic many years before, Tschirner's pistol, which had been confiscated by Dhobi at the time of the landing and a recent picture of the Junkers. Lawless watched the items being sealed into a tin box and rose, swaying like a mighty tree in a tropical storm. One hand reached out to seize it. With one more defiant look around the table he lumbered from the clubhouse, almost tearing the door from its hinges as he walked off into the night. The bemused silence was broken by the sound of a bulldozer engine being gunned and the rattle and screech of steel tracks.

Everyone made a dash for the door and spilled outside in fear as they saw the huge yellow machine, headlights blazing, rattling and roaring towards them with Lawless at the controls.

Twenty yards away Lawless tugged at a lever sending the bulldozer veering wildly towards the clubhouse's corner.

'Jesus Christ, he's lost his marbles! He's going to knock the bloody clubhouse down!' The member who had made the observation about church walls was suddenly sobered.

With Lawless frantically and erratically tugging at its levers, the machine lurched back towards the clubhouse's entrance before fixing on its original target and engaging with the corner in a splintering of wood and brickwork. Lawless's incoherent bellowing could be heard even above the bulldozer's roar as it backed off before resuming its assault with its blade lowered. A deep furrow of earth now ended under a sagging eave.

None of the members, least of all Hollywood, felt like stopping Lawless. Hesitantly, like a dog sniffing a dead rabbit, the bulldozer backed off and stood still with its engine running as Lawless jumped from the cab clutching the box in which the mementoes had been placed. Alice ran towards Lawless and kissed him. Two bare arms enfolded her and they stood together for a moment.

Gently he released her, kissed her and placed the box in the hole.

The very worst thing BOLLOX residents could have done at that precise moment was to cheer. Twenty or so young men and women, aroused by the prospect of damage and violence, were clinging to the boundary fence like monkeys, shouting and jeering.

Without even appearing to have seen or heard them, Lawless climbed back into the cab, gunned the throttle and with a throw of the steering levers spun the machine round.

'GOOD BUY AND GOOD RIDDUNSE' was caught in the bulldozer's lights as the blade trashed the first of the concrete posts and mangled the heavy wire netting. Lights were coming on all over the complex, the occupants alerted by shouts.

Like a knight's visor the blade dropped and struck where the word 'riddunse' had been sprayed. A horizontal split erupted in the building's flank and the wall began to fold along its line.

Smaller and younger BOLLOX residents were trampled or shoved aside by older and bigger delinquents seeking safety as the bulldozer punched at the main building with a relentless rhythm.

'Stop the mad bugger! Call for the fuzz, someone!' a BOLLOX teacher screamed without realizing that all telephone lines had been torn away in the first onslaught.

Lawless had by now mastered the subtleties of the bulldozer controls and was selecting his next target. He backed away for a moment, surveying the scene like a fighting bull deciding where to make its next charge. A Citroen 2CV sporting Nuclear Power No Thanks and Meat is Murder stickers was caught in the headlights for several seconds before being scooped up by the bulldozer's blade.

Bearing his booty aloft in malicious triumph Lawless turned the machine towards the most substantial-looking wall and slammed the car into all that remained of BOLLOX's central accommodation block.

With the car reduced to tinsel and the main block now a fair imitation of Hiroshima on the worst day in its history, Lawless pressed home his attack on some of the smaller buildings.

Looting began almost immediately. Anything of value was being snatched from the wreckage and bundled into cars, which were immediately jemmied by other residents and the stolen contents spirited away.

'Someone's bound to have raised the alarm!' Dhobi shouted imploringly at Alice. 'We'll have to get him away from that thing before the coppers arrive.'

An idea had formed in Dhobi's mind. Not a particularly subtle one, but effective. The brain that had masterminded the transformation on paper of a twin-engined bomber into a humble woodworking tool was at work again. Sirens were howling in the distance.

Dhobi smiled a wicked little grin as he watched three youths smash the window of a teacher's estate car and remove the stolen property from within.

Even as the police cars and an armed response vehicle screeched past the old guardroom and slewed to a halt near the scene of destruction, half a dozen yobs were trying to pull a safe away from the ruins. Others who had been beaten to the booty or who had lost interest in plunder contented themselves with heaving half-bricks at a knot of older teachers who stood miserably by.

'Armed police! Cease what you are doing immediately and step out into the light with your hands where we can see them!' The loudspeaker command barked out over the desolated scene.

In line with the force's equality policies the warning was repeated in Welsh, Hindi, Gujarati and Rap.

'Stop all de fightin' and the stealin' and de lyin',
Cos de fuzz doan wanna see de poor dudes dyin''

Was the rap version shouted out by one of the officers of the Mobile Urban Detection and Further Community Affirmative Action Squad (MUDAFUCAS) who had arrived in a large van of their own and already set up a Mobile Arrest Trauma Centre.

As police began the task of rounding up the BOLLOX pupils, the Maescwm Flying Club members slipped quietly inside their clubhouse as though nothing of any special interest had happened.

By the time an inspector and sergeant had introduced themselves, Lawless was innocently standing at the bar.

'I'm Inspector Luff and this is Sergeant Cleat. We are here in connection with a serious incident involving criminal damage and the theft of a vehicle, namely a Caterpillar tractor,' Luff announced to Dhobi.

'By persons known or unknown?' Megan piped up, her voice sweet with innocence.

'Unknown,' Inspector Luff snapped. 'As yet,' and sent a withering glance round the room.

Dhobi's pulse raced with momentary panic. Even the thickest member of the local force could hardly fail to notice that Lawless was covered from head to foot in cement dust, and put two and two together. He would have to play his trump card quickly.

'Perhaps, Inspector, we could have a word. In private?'

Inspector Luff grunted his assent. Dhobi led him away from the bar and Lawless and towards the settee, over which hung the portrait of Joystick Morgan. Luff lowered his considerable bulk into the settee, looking out through the gaping hole in the clubhouse's corner into the clamorous night.

Dhobi looked up at the picture of Joystick and began to whisper a prayer before remembering that to have Joystick Morgan on your side was lethal. Sergeant Cleat, Dhobi noticed, was being worked on by Megan who had provided coffee and was now moving in heavily and transparently with the flirtation. Lawless had been ushered to the washroom by Alice and had reappeared with the dust brushed from his person.

Through the gap in the wall Luff could see a crop of BOLLOX youths being processed by MUDAFUCAS. Some others were already being counselled in the Mobile Arrest Trauma caravan by three policewomen with sociology degrees. From somewhere outside his vision but within his hearing, came the screams of other youths being enthusiastically counselled by some of the older coppers using a more traditional approach.

At the sound of their yelps Luff smiled for the first time.

Dhobi and Luff conferred for half an hour until approaching eleven o'clock when a cry went out from Megan which had never before been heard within the portals of Maescwm Flying Club.

'Time, ladies and gentlemen, please! Let me have your glasses! I shall naturally order a taxi for any member who feels he or she has imbibed over the legal blood alcohol limit, but I must ask you to drink up. The law is the law!'

Luff beamed approval but Sergeant Cleat, who had on two previous occasions been a club guest, looked baffled. Luff and Dhobi shook hands and took their formal parting. Members were shrugging themselves into their coats as Megan whisked a brush around the floor and began to up-end the seats onto tables.

Cleat looked around, his suspicions aroused. Nothing he could put his finger on. Just . . . odd. As though a charade were being enacted.

He sniffed as a howl of agony came from outside.

A constable who was a tighthead prop in the Wales Police rugby squad was counselling a youth who had referred to him as reactionary fascist pig. Luff was beckoning him away from the bar. If the boss wasn't unduly suspicious then he wasn't going to make waves. Especially as he had recognized one of the club members as being an influential local magistrate.

Giving Megan one last lingering and meaningful look, Cleat bade those remaining a curt good night and left in Luff's wake.

Taxis had indeed arrived. Any mystification as to the sudden outburst of lawfulness among members was dispelled when the cab drivers saw police moving among the wreckage of BOLLOX like an occuping army flushing out snipers.

'This is a bloody turn-up for the book. We'd be out of business if we relied on you lot being taken home after a night's boozing,' observed Dai Prosser as he ferried one member away from the chaotic scene. Much as he would liked to have lingered to see exactly what was going on, his concern that the police might not share his own liberal view of the vehicle excise licence laws was greater than his curiosity.

Lawless slipped his arm around Alice and stumbled off quietly.

Megan finished her sweeping up, whisked a wet cloth over the bar and shouted a reminder to Dhobi to lock up.

Only Hollywood and Dhobi remained.

Hollywood had been eavesdropping. All in all it had been quite a night for eaves being dropped.

'I was watching every move he made. Not an eyelash moved without me noticing and, believe me, you were laying it on with a trowel.' Hollywood poured two large drinks and offered one with a knowing smile.

'Tell Hollywood. What did you say to that big butch policeman?'

Dhobi sniffed his brandy appreciatively and swirled it in the glass.

'I was helping Mr Luff with his enquiries. As a public-spirited citizen I felt it necessary to inform him as to who was driving the bulldozer.'

'You did WHAT?'

Hollywood's voice was a screech. His face whitened.

'I don't believe you! Lawless looked like the abominable snowman under all that dust! Even Alice would have been hard put to recognize him! And you *told* them it was Lawless?'

'Who said anything about Lawless?'

Dhobi took his drink away from his lips. The look was one of feigned innocence but his eyes twinkled mischief. 'When those two policemen arrived Lawless was at the bar, was he not, innocently enjoying a drink in the company of his wife and friends?'

'Yes. But only because someone had got him away in time. I saw what I saw. It was Lawless who levelled BOL-LOX. Everybody saw it.'

Dhobi beamed.

'The BOLLOX people didn't. They only came out once the bulldozer had started. The machine's lights shining outwards would have made it impossible to see who was in the cab. I for one am prepared to swear it was Greaser in that cab.'

'You old tinker. Don't tell me . . . Yes, do.'

Dhobi cast his eyes round the room which was dark apart from one light above them which had been left on.

'Just you and me? Secrets?'

'For God's sake, yes. Secrets.'

'Well. You saw the BOLLOX crew looting the building, did you not?'

'Everybody did. They were blatant.'

'Blatant, indeed. And careless. I happened to overhear a couple of yobs preparing to take some of the stolen stuff to Greaser's garage. They were away for about half an hour, so my guess was they'd managed to stash it there. Naturally it was my duty to inform Inspector Luff of what I had overheard. Some police were sent to check the premises and there it was.'

'So they'll nick him for receiving. Greaser will then sing like a canary about the Junkers, Tschirner, Lang and McNally and we'll all be behind bars. Excuse me if I don't sound very impressed.' Hollywood lit a lime green cocktail cigarette and smoked in angry, short snatches.

Dhobi drank thoughtfully. Hollywood looked disgusted.

'He'll sing. But nobody will listen.'

'Oh?'

Dhobi drank slowly, letting Hollywood stew.

'Oh, yes. You see, the police know that it was a Junkers that bombed the bunker and are ninety-nine per cent certain that it took off from here. But they won't do anything. Orders. Coming right from the top.'

'I can't begin to understand.'

'That's because you don't know the official mind. Look. The RAF has been caught with its pants down. An ancient World War II bomber has taken off inside the airspace they are supposed to be protecting and blown up a target with a sodding great bomb.

'Now if the culprits could be traced all well and good. Their inefficiency would be covered up and the guilty parties brought to trial but . . .'

'But none of the people in the plane actually existed?'

'My point exactly. Any Minister of Defence who stood up in the House of Commons to answer questions about an ancient Jerry bomber crewed by non-existent men would be out of a job. So, no questions are going to be asked. End of story.'

Hollywood exhaled, still doubtful.

'But I don't believe the RAF could be so . . . well . . . silly.'

'I can,' said Dhobi, remembering the time when a bomber was changed from a 'Plane, German' into a 'Plane, Carpentry.'

'Never underestimate the ponderous inefficiency of the bureaucratic mind,' said Hollywood and clinked glasses with Dhobi.

'To the memory of Tschirner and Lang. The best invisible chums an old RAF flying station could ever have!'

Chapter Twenty-two

TIME-SERVED MECHANIC, APPLY WITHIN.

And then in Welsh underneath.

The garage was a wartime Quonset hut off the metalled B road. An ancient tin sign screwed to the flaking concrete frontage advertised National Benzole petrol although McNally guessed the sign had been placed there to mend the wall.

There were two petrol pumps of antique design and a little wooden kiosk with nobody in attendance. His arrival, since it was on foot, was unannounced by any automatic bell.

An eviscerated Land Rover of early 1970s vintage occupied much of the front of the workshop but he could also see a very old car, which he thought might be a Wolseley, right at the back.

Gaskets to fit engines which had been out of production for thirty years or more and lengths of cable and piping hung from nails in the wall. Every flat surface was overflowing with starter motors, generators, pistons and their connecting-rods, grease guns, old cans and bottles of unspecified oleaginous substances, all of them covered with a heavy, grey patina of dust.

A light shone at a cluttered workbench over which an old man was hunched, making slow and even strokes with a file. After a few moments the old man took his work from the vice and checked it with a micrometer. He had to peer hard through his thick horn-rimmed spectacles at the tiny gradations which he read off out loud.

He turned and over the top of his glasses caught sight of McNally and smiled.

Even before he advanced towards the old man to ask for the job, McNally knew that, for the time being at least, he was home.